# IN THE SHADOW OF SALEM

## A Novel
## Inspired by True Events

by
### DONNA B. GAWELL

HERITAGE BEACON
F I C T I O N

IN THE SHADOW OF SALEM BY DONNA B. GAWELL
Published by Heritage Beacon Fiction
an imprint of Lighthouse Publishing of the Carolinas
2333 Barton Oaks Dr., Raleigh, NC, 27614

ISBN: 978-1-946016-50-8
Copyright © 2018 by Donna B. Gawell
Cover design by Elaina Lee
Interior design by AtriTeX Technologies P Ltd

Available in print from your local bookstore, online, or from the publisher at:
ShopLPC.com

For more information on this book and the author visit: www.DonnaGawell.com

This is a fictional account of the life of Mehitabel Braybrooke Downing, based on the seventeenth-century historical town and court records from Essex County, Massachusetts. Some of the names, characters, and incidents are products of the author's imagination or are used for fictional purposes. Any mentioned brand names, places, and trademarks remain the property of their respective owners, bear no association with the author or the publisher, and are used for fictional purposes only.

Scripture quotations from The Authorized (King James) Version. Rights in the Authorized Version in the United Kingdom are vested in the Crown. Reproduced by permission of the Crown's patentee, Cambridge University Press.

Brought to you by the creative team at Lighthouse Publishing of the Carolinas:
Eddie Jones, Ann Tatlock, Jerri Menges, Shonda Savage, Elaina Lee, Brian Cross

Library of Congress Cataloging-in-Publication Data
Gawell, Donna B.
In the Shadow of Salem / Donna B. Gawell 1st edition.

Printed in the United States of America

# DEDICATION

This book is dedicated to my husband, Mark, who after listening to me retell Mehitabel's amazing life story about a thousand times to anyone who would listen, encouraged me to sit down and write this novel.

# Acknowledgements

I wish to express my sincere thanks and appreciation to the many people who offered guidance, information, encouragement, and reviews during the research and writing of this novel. Special appreciation is given to two historians. Richard Trask is the town archivist for Danvers (formerly Salem Village) and a leading authority on the Salem Witchcraft trials of 1692. Mr. Trask provided me with recently uncovered resources relating to Mehitabel and Joan's imprisonment during the trials. He also pointed me to valuable resources as I researched. Gordon Harris, the renowned Ipswich historian, offered encouragement and information about the seventeenth-century colonists and early colonial history for Ipswich, Massachusetts. Gordon's website, historicipswich.org, is a local and historical treasure.

Many people came alongside me as I edited and revised. Jerri Menges, my content editor, patiently and meticulously helped me craft this novel into a story of which I am very proud. Ann Tatlock, my managing editor, offered encouragement from the first moment my manuscript was submitted and guided me through the curious and sometimes confusing process of publishing. Early on, MaryAnne Haffner and Laurie Penner offered numerous editing and suggestions in revision.

My appreciation is also extended to the many people in my life who inspired some of the more noble characters in the story. I hope my pastor, Steve Benninger, and his wife, Shirley, discover glimpses of themselves in Reverend William and Mistress Margaret Hubbard.

My gratitude goes out over the centuries past to Mehitabel Braybrooke. This book would never have been written if not for the records left because of her remarkable and challenging life.

My husband, Mark, continually supported and encouraged me during my research and writing, and was patient during the times I needed solitude to focus on finishing a scene. My on-site research in New England was made possible because of his love and dedication. His companionship and help in the libraries, museums, graveyards, and historical centers made the adventure a pleasure.

# INTRODUCTION

*In the Shadow of Salem* takes place in Ipswich, Massachusetts, not long after the "Great Migration" period in colonial America (1620-1640). Ipswich sat "in the shadow" between Salem Village (now Danvers) and the town of Salem, and was closely connected to both—socially and politically. The impact of the Salem Witchcraft Trials reached throughout the Massachusetts Bay Colony, as the majority of those accused were imprisoned in Salem, Ipswich, and Boston.

The Puritans, who settled in the areas near Boston, were an English sect of Christians who arrived in the American colonies in the 1630s. Not to be confused with the Pilgrims of Plymouth, who wished to separate completely from the Church of England, the Puritans hoped to purify the corrupt church.

In England, Puritans were often people of means, political influence, and were well educated, but King Charles would not tolerate their ministers' attempts to reform the Church. As persecution mounted and the prospects of a civil war loomed, many chose to leave England and establish a colony whose government, society, and church were based solely on the Bible.

There are a few terms unique to the era of this story for which an explanation might be helpful.

**Goody, Goodwife,** and **Goodman:** The Puritans used these terms to address married members of their congregations. *Mister* and *Mistress* were reserved for the more elite members of the Puritan community.

**King Phillip's War:** An armed conflict between native Indian inhabitants in New England and English colonists and their Indian allies in 1675–78. King Phillip was the name of the Indian chief of the Wampanoag people.

**Massachusetts Bay Colony:** One of the original English settlements in present-day Massachusetts settled in 1630 by a group of about 1,000 Puritans from England under Governor John Winthrop.

**Meetinghouse:** The central building in the early colonies used for both church services and court.

**Ordinary:** Another name for taverns in the 1600s.

**Pilgrims (Separatists):** The first colonists in Plymouth, who wished to separate from the Church of England.

**Specter:** An invisible spirit who could only be seen by the afflicted. Most Puritans believed that a witch's specter could torment its victims and that others might not witness the event. The Salem Witchcraft Trials allowed spectral evidence as testimony.

**Tithingman:** A churchman assigned to keep discipline in the congregation during church services and in daily living.

**Witchcraft**: The Puritans carried the fervent belief in the existence of witchcraft from Europe to the colonies. It would have been odd and even heretical to believe that witches did not exist. Those found guilty were hung or, in the case of Giles Corey, pressed to death by stones. The burning of witches was a punishment in Europe, not the colonies.

# Chapter One

# September 21, 1692

The lock on the door of the Ipswich prison clanged, and the bar raised to open it. No good news ever came when we heard those creaking hinges at the top of the stairs. Unwelcome breezes from outdoors stirred the poisonous stench of dung from the corners of our cell. The dark shadows at sunset did not allow me to recognize the woman flanked by the guards in the doorway, but old Goody Vinson could see her. "Mehitabel," she whispered, "you will not believe who has come to join us!"

Joan Penney's voice raged throughout the dungeon as she was hurtled down the stairs by the two night guards. They showed little respect for the elderly woman, and she stumbled on the last step. In disgust, the guards allowed her to fall onto the filthy straw floor. Her eyes were downcast as she hobbled over to sit with the older women.

A heavy silence fell over us, until Rachel Clinton spoke, "Joan, we have been expecting you. Soon all of the townswomen will be here to replace those already hung in the gallows. Look, even your daughter is here. Are your eyes so weak you don't see her face?"

Rachel's loathsome manner was unwelcomed by all. "Mehitabel, go to your mother," she commanded me. "Share your warm blanket with her."

I moved close to Joan to silence the foolishness of Rachel Clinton, although I knew my presence would only add to my stepmother's humiliation. Surely Joan knew she would find me amongst the prisoners. She must have known about the accusation of witchcraft, that I had been waiting for my trial in this dingy prison for the last three months. Joan never sent any food or a single word of comfort.

"Joan, are you accused of witchcraft?" I uttered with as much compassion as I could muster. "Who accused you?"

"Zebulon Hill!" Joan glanced around, noting that even the most feeble had made their way closer to hear her story. She proceeded in a stoic tone, "He said I had cast an affliction on his daughter, Mary. The old scoundrel knows Thomas' children will reward him handsomely if they can take the farm their father left to me. Scoundrels, all!" Joan spat on the ground in front of her and continued, "We have had many quarrels about these matters, and now I am here."

Joan's marriage to Thomas Penney, a year after Father's death, brought her only grief with his children, and they were now beyond angry at the reading of his will. He had left almost everything to Joan. Widows like her, who had no sons or brothers to look out for their interests, were easy prey for the ruthless. If Joan stayed in prison for any length of time, Thomas Penney's children would gain power over her entire estate, and she would leave this dank cell penniless.

"Mehitabel, I tell you, nothing I said to the courts made any difference to my fate. I even said the Lord's Prayer without error! When I ended it, I added that I also forgave all who trespassed against me. Not one error in my prayer! My fate was the same as George Burroughs or anyone else who recited the Lord's Prayer without error. We are all here because of the greed of Satan. People are becoming rich from our estates, and our farms are being seized and sold. While we are sitting here, Thomas' children are selling off all I own!"

The other prisoners, most being strangers, knew little of the stories Joan or I might tell. Even those who thought they were friends were blind to the truth. My family's desire to present the illusion of piety could never sit astride a fence. Surely some had heard the distorted snippets from those villagers who despised our family or simply loved the art of gossip. Truth had been but a stranger here in Ipswich these past forty years.

My hands managed to caress Joan's, and she looked into my eyes. Our miserable fates were bound together in this vile pit of Hell in Ipswich. But our miserable fate had begun a long time before then …

# CHAPTER TWO

# 1656

I was four when I first heard the word *bastard*. Mother had just returned from a trip to Ipswich, and she blazed into the house like a fierce winter storm. She glared at me and then turned to Father and screamed, "I was made to believe that we would never see your whoring serving girl again!"

Father's eyes widened. He grabbed Mother's arm and forced her into a chair near the fire. Her reddish face was evil, her eyes cold and flinty, her lips pursed. Father glanced at me with consternation, and with authority not typical of him, said, "Mehitabel, go to your room and wait there until I come for you."

Frightened, I scampered up the stairs but kept the door open a crack. Even if it had been closed, I would still have heard the rage in Mother's voice. "Richard, you sent your harlot to Topsfield, but she has returned to Ipswich as a married woman! I have fed and clothed your bastard child, and people have come to think of me as her mother. Now, with your whore in town, the neighbors will never let my shame be put to rest."

Mother's voice weakened, and she sounded close to tears. I could barely hear Father's voice: "Joan, I am deeply sorry for the sorrow my sin has brought to you and Mehitabel. I'm so sorry ... so sorry ... I beg your forgiveness."

Mother returned to her rage. "I have no forgiveness for you or *your* child. Mehitabel is a curse on my heart." Her voice quieted as tears choked her words. "I can't understand why God has punished me with barrenness. I suffer under this curse, which started with your whore. She is the one who has set a curse upon me that did not allow me to have my own child. It has been a cruel fate and punishment that I was forced by the court to raise Mehitabel. You and your whore may have been whipped, but I am the one who lives under Mehitabel's curse every day."

For a few moments, all I could hear were sobs, from both parents. Eventually, Father spoke, his voice calm and comforting. "Joan, we must go on as husband and wife, but we must also find a way to be gentle with Mehitabel. She is just an innocent, forced to suffer under this curse."

"No, Richard! I will do what I must to keep this accursed child in our home, but it is your responsibility to care for her soul and spirit, not mine." The door blasted open, and everything went silent.

Father was sitting by the fire on my stool when I descended the stairs to see if anyone was still in the house. His hands enveloped his face and then slid down his cheeks when he heard my footsteps.

"Father, what has happened? Where is Mother?"

"Come sit with me, my darling Mehitabel." Father removed my coif and stroked my long curls as he also tried to dry the tears from my eyes. "Mother has stepped out for a while. Please know that I love you dearly and will try to be a better father to you. I know … how deeply Mother's words must hurt you, but there are some things you are too young to understand. You are the apple of my eye, just as God thinks we are all the apple of His eyes. I love you as much."

Later that evening, the still night air was awakened by the sound of footsteps. I looked up from my slate as the outside door creaked, announcing Mother's return. She hung her cape on the hook near the fireplace and walked straight to her chair without speaking a word to me. Father was tending to his nighttime chores in the barn.

*Perhaps Mother is in a better mood*, I thought. *Maybe I can do something to make her happy with me.*

"Mother, there is stew in the kettle. Can I bring you some?"

She said nothing, so I sat on the ground near the hearth as the thick wood crackled and the bright flames slowly ate away at it. Mother's eyes gazed at the glowing embers. How I yearned for her embrace, to sit on her lap and put my cheek to hers.

I stood and walked to the cupboard and fetched a cup of rum. I placed a thick slice of bread for Mother on her treasured pewter plate and came back to her side.

"Here, Mother," I held out the plate. "You must be hungry."

Mother sipped the rum and frowned. "Mehitabel! This rum is cold, and the bread is dry. You ruin everything you touch. Just go away from me!" Without bothering to find my cape, I dashed out the door to find Father.

I had always known Mother had no tender feelings for me. She did not care for me the same way I saw other mothers love their children. I was not allowed to speak to her except to offer to do a chore.

I knew my father's love was certain, but the dark clouds that accompanied Mother were an ever-present part of my life, causing a growing anger in me. If only my father hadn't committed the sin of fornication … if only I had been the child of a first or second wife instead of his indentured servant girl, maybe Mother would have found some love for me. Instead, my constant childhood companions were her angry probes and steely silences. I learned to keep my fury to myself and cried tears of shame for my father's sin.

## CHAPTER THREE

# 1656

Nathaniel Rogers must have lamented the winter snows still on the ground in early April as he moved with a quick gait down the muddy path to the meetinghouse. Unlike some ministers who chose to arrive late in order to make an entrance, Nathaniel, cloaked with his usual somber demeanor, was usually the earliest person to enter.

Standing at the door's entrance reading the posts was his good friend, Emanuel Downing. Mr. Downing held an elite circle of friends in Ipswich. With his hands clasped behind his back, he stood like a buck with large antlers, exuding his customary air of gravitas.

Father gripped my hand tightly, and I shivered with each step as we walked toward the two esteemed men. Father bowed with a respectful nod to both Reverend Rogers and Mr. Downing, and we were about to continue our steps when Mr. Downing abruptly grasped Father's shoulder. "Richard, would you please stay here for just a moment while I conclude my conversation with our minister? I wish to speak with you about an urgent matter."

Emanuel turned back to Reverend Rogers and continued their exchange. "Nathaniel, I have something of great importance to discuss with you after the meeting. Would you come to my home after the morning service and be our honored guest at our midday meal?" Nathaniel Rogers seemed to enjoy comradery with his dear friend who had been nothing but supportive and had helped appoint him to the ministry in Ipswich. Emanuel added, "Please bring your wife, Margaret, as my request also concerns her."

"Yes, of course. We will come right after services. Margaret and I always feel blessed to be your guests." Reverend Rogers entered the meetinghouse and then closed the door tightly to guard against the devilish winds.

Emanuel Downing's manner today was tense and focused as if he had an important mission to accomplish. He turned to my father. "Richard, you and I came to Ipswich near the same year, and I have learned to trust your judgment concerning the crops and animals you manage so well. I will be leaving Ipswich soon to return to England. My wife will accompany me this time, and I am asking you to oversee my lands until my attorneys can procure a new owner."

Father stood taller at this request. It was evident his appointment to the town courts this past year elevated him in the eyes of such a distinguished and learned man as Emanuel Downing. Father had always been recognized as a man of distinction in his own right, being made a freeman by Master Dennison soon after his arrival. As a freeman, he was given the right and responsibility to have significant involvement in Ipswich's business and legal affairs. Emanuel's request would provide further evidence Father was an esteemed citizen of Ipswich.

"Mr. Downing, I will do all I can to serve you and your family in your absence. I consider it an honor, sir."

"Richard, I am certain we will not be returning to the colony, even though we have prospered greatly and share friendship with so many esteemed and godly people here in Ipswich. My reasons are many, but Lucy wants to return to London as she lives in terror with the heinous stories of attacks from the savages."

Father sighed and strummed his fingers on his chest. "Aye, so many reports. Just yesterday, a woman in Topsfield told of an Indian named Nimrod who came into her home with others, and she felt he was there to do her much harm. He has been arrested and will be tried next session. The entire town does, indeed, have much to fear."

"Lucy seeks to spend our remaining years with our son George and his children in London, in a more comfortable setting." Emanuel exuded his usual air of confidence, and Father may have imagined Emanuel had likely secured the promise of a royal position in the courts.

I could no longer hold my tongue. "But, Mr. Downing! Please don't go! I can't bear never to see John and Robin again!" Tears welled up in my eyes.

"Ah, Mistress Mehitabel. I can see you would miss John's mischief during the sermons when the tithingman scolds him with his stick," said Emanuel with a pleasant smile.

"That is true, but I also like to watch John and his brothers whisper to one another and see them laugh when no one else takes notice. John always makes faces at me."

"Don't worry, dear child. John will hopefully be cared for by our Reverend Rogers." Emanuel then turned back to address my father. "My children born in Ipswich, I fear, would not do well in London society. You understand, Richard … you came from the motherland."

Assured that John would not leave Ipswich with his parents, I broke into a huge smile, twirled, and promptly tumbled onto the snowy ground but sprang back up.

"I'm not hurt!" I reassured them.

Emanuel smiled, but then his voice took on a somber tone. "Richard, I also must ask that you tell no one about this until tomorrow. Nathaniel and I have many details to discuss, and only a few townspeople are aware of my departure. I need your discretion. My attorneys will be by to visit this week to discuss your compensation and responsibilities.

"Now, I must move along. Good day, Goodman Braybrooke." Emanuel began his ascent into the meetinghouse but then turned to address me only. He put his finger to his lips and with a stern grin looked squarely at me. "Mehitabel, I ask you not to say a word, or I shall send John and Robin over to chastise you!"

My face lit up, and quickly Emanuel probably realized a visit from his sons was just what I had hoped. *Oh, that John Downing would ever come to my home,* I recall wishing at the tender age of four.

# CHAPTER FOUR

# 1665

The winter of 1665 finally began to fade. Mayflowers emerged in the nearby woods, and skunk cabbages revealed their pungent sprouts. Their forest fragrances invited skilled healers to explore the woods for plants and pods for their medicines.

"Mehitabel, find my baskets and sacks," Mother instructed me one crisp spring morning. "Today will be a fine day to search for newly sprouted herbs. My knees no longer allow me to bend down to reach the plants, so it is high time for you to learn. Maybe you can be of some help for once."

"I am thirteen, Mother! I would love to help you." I scurried about the house selecting baskets and woven bags. "I've watched carefully, so I know which baskets and knives are your favorites."

We walked past Mother's prized garden, carefully closing the rough wooden gate that seemed as big as a heifer. Tendrils of ivy grew in every direction and cascaded over the fence as if to warn the creatures of the forests that this garden was forbidden. Mother's herbs and healing plants were of greater importance than any vegetable we might eat, especially the borage and angelica for her melancholy.

I twirled down the path to the woods, enjoying the sun's warmth. Mother hobbled along and gritted her teeth to mask the pain, and we soon reached the edge of the forest. The air was heavy with the smell of the new season's leaves and blooms mixed with the ever-present dampness of the forest. An occasional bird flitted from branch to branch, and three squirrels rustled the dry brown leaves on the forest floor as they dashed up a nearby trunk.

Mother pushed aside the brambles and small branches with her walking stick so we could see. "The first thing you must know is that some of the loveliest plants can be deadly. Look here at the jack-in-the-pulpit. Touch it, and you will have blisters. Eat the berries or the roots, and you will have sores inside your mouth and down your throat. But watch. If I put this rag around the roots to protect my hand, I can harvest the roots and cook them for a cure for coughs and headaches. See, it is safe if cooked. The Indians chop up the raw taproot and mix it with meat to leave out for their enemies, who can't even taste the poison."

A fallen pine blocked our way as we wandered deeper into the woods. I deftly leaped over it and offered my arm to steady Mother's approach.

The sun flickered down to illuminate an open area covered by a small field. "Mother, look at these pretty plants, with red jewels for flowers."

"See, you are beginning to understand how the plants are named," she responded. "People call these the Jewel Weed. The leaves are used to make a poultice for skin irritations."

My heart danced at the thought that perhaps Mother could see I had a talent for identifying healing herbs and plants. Whenever she saw a healing plant, she stopped and explained its usefulness. The forest was my school, and she was my teacher.

I recited my list of newly learned cures over and over on our walk home. "Linden leaves to make tea for headaches, witch hazel bark for coughs, tamarack bark for sores and burns …"

At one point, I turned to her. "Mother, I hope that someday people will come to me for healing, just like they now come to you. Tomorrow, you can teach me about the herbs in your garden."

Mother's demeanor transformed from calm to irritation. "You are not to touch those, Mehitabel! I don't even let our serving girls care for those. Healing gardens such as mine have been carefully tended, and I want *no* one in there. Weed the cabbage, beans, lettuce, and turnips, but not my herbs. I have enough problems with the creatures helping themselves; I don't need *you* to ruin my plants."

The lovely day suddenly became one of disappointment. I knew Mother's garden on the south side of our home was one of the most bountiful and respected in Ipswich. Still, her words stung like the hairs of nettle.

During the next few weeks, Mother allowed me to go into the woods without her to scrounge for her treasures. I spent long days securing plants, hoping to please her, and she inspected my baskets upon my return. May into June brought dry, warm days, and my forays into the woods were a welcome respite from the usual chores of planting crops.

Father cautioned me never to venture far into the forest, which he feared was infested with savages. Servants received a few extra shillings to protect me, and they would hunt for hazelnuts while I foraged through the riches of the woodlands. These were the happiest times of my childhood, and Mother's conditional approbation warmed me further.

Late June brought torrential rains with intense heat and the whirl of thick, moist winds. The storms pelted our crops with hail, and their winds blew the thatch off part of the barn, but they also delivered an unwelcome arrival who would forever change my destiny.

The muted crack of distant thunder mixed with an ominous knock at our door one afternoon. Mother signaled me to move away from the entrance while she opened the door. A gaunt man dressed in a tattered brown waistcoat and large brimmed hat stood at the entryway. Mother rubbed the back of her neck with her hand and glared at the man instead of extending a greeting. Her irritated demeanor caused him to take a step backward before politely removing his hat.

"Goodwife Braybrooke? My name is John Allen. I'm a minister from Dedham. I bring you greetings but also some most unfortunate news. Might I speak with your husband, Richard?" Reverend Allen's hands shook as he struggled to present a dignified and compassionate appearance.

"You and your serving boy may sit at the table while a servant fetches my husband. He is far out in the fields," Mother replied with little graciousness or hospitality for our weary visitors.

Reverend Allen wrung his hands together and glanced around as if hoping a more hospitable person would appear. "My good woman, this boy is not a servant. This is John Beare, your husband's nephew. John has informed me that he has never met you since he arrived in the colony."

"True, I have never laid eyes on him. Well, sit anyway, and I will have our servant fetch Richard." Mother's cold eyes peered down at them. She pivoted to face the door but stood just a moment before she opened the latch, breathing a heavy sigh of annoyance. Whatever news the minister was to deliver would surely bring misery to Mother. She then left the house without another word.

I had strained to hear the few words spoken as I peered from the side room. Quiet as a curious tabby cat, I stepped out to study Father's kin. The boy was a full head taller than I but close in age. John's skin and hair had a reddish tint, with old man lines sketched on his forehead. He rested with a bag clutched close to his side, his countenance glum for a youth.

The good reverend sprang to his feet. "Young miss, I'm sorry. I didn't notice you when we came into the house."

I bent my knees slightly to show respect and then stood behind Father's best chair.

"I welcome you both. Sir, I met John briefly last summer, when Father took me to Dedham to meet his parents." I turned to John. "Where is your father? Is he well?"

John sat with a vacant stare and arms crossed. He turned his head toward me and imparted this grievous news: "My father is dead." Each word that came from his mouth was chopped from the other in a somber and angry tone. He turned back to glare at the fire and said no more. Realizing that my common sense had not judged the situation properly, I fell silent.

Reverend Allen fumbled with the parchment from his satchel. He pretended to read his documents, but I could see his eyes did not follow any lines on the paper.

The sound of footsteps signaled Father's arrival, and his heavy breathing revealed he had run the entire way from the hay fields. Mother followed behind, the grim look of annoyance still covering her face.

"Reverend Allen, I have not made your acquaintance, but I welcome you into my house. Joan, please tend to the men's hunger and thirst. John, my boy, it has been since July I saw you last."

Stone-faced, Mother slipped out the door to find our servants Peter or Mary to tend to the guests. Reverend Allen rose to greet Father, then all gathered at the table. With a broad smile, Father glanced at John Beare. "John, you must have grown a head's length since I last saw you. You look so healthy and well."

I was still standing by the hearth. "Mehitabel, come join us. You haven't seen John for a year. Has it been since last summer?"

John spoke not a word. The reverend interrupted. "Richard, we have some grave news. Ezekiel, John's father, has died of smallpox. You must have heard about the outbreak north of Salem. He was overtaken with it while on a trading expedition. John has been with my wife and me since that time as he has no kin in Dedham. I knew you would gladly take John in as your own. Your dear departed sister would have wished it to be so. Certainly, a man without a son to help on the farm would greatly benefit from such a fine young man as John."

I had expected my father to be at least a bit distressed to hear he would have another child to raise. He struggled to find time to listen to my lessons as of late; surely, another person to feed and care for would be a significant burden. Instead, his face widened with a huge, welcoming smile, and he planted his hands on John's shoulder.

"John, as your uncle, I know your parents would be deeply pleased and grateful if you made your home with us. Yes, it will be good, very good to have a young man to help with the many chores and responsibilities I have on this farm." Father continued to rub John's shoulders with the embrace of one who is familiar and family.

John Beare's countenance brightened with Father's warm welcome. "Thank you, Uncle. I hope to learn from you and to be of help."

John turned to look at me, his mouth crooked. "Mehitabel, we will no longer be cousins but closer, like brother and sister." Only I could see the scowl on his face.

I startled when John Beare said he would be like my brother. I had always wanted an older brother, but one more amiable, like John or Robin Downing. How grand it would be to have a caring older brother who protected me or teased me at church meetings!

Father acknowledged Reverend Allen's departure, and then he turned to John Beare. "Well, let's assess what is in order. I have been talking to Joan about someday adding to this house, and now you have presented me a reason to do so."

"Uncle, I have been to homes in Salem somewhat larger than this and recall how the rooms were built. I shall look forward to assisting you," John replied.

That night, many thoughts wandered through my mind. *Father will have much less time for me, but perhaps Mother will see that having John in our home could be to her advantage. John might make the house happier because Father's life will be easier.*

For the first time, a more hideous thought occurred to me. *Could it be that my plight as Father's only child had been a burden he had kept hidden?* The Scriptures were clear that a son was the one who blesses a parent. I had been such a disappointment in so many ways but thought I was only a curse to Mother. Now, it was evident I was an albatross and a wretched curse to my father as well.

# CHAPTER FIVE

# 1666

Our much grander residence was lovely, with a second story that hung over the original structure. Sparkling diamond-camed windows gave it a charming expression. Shadows from the towering oaks sheltered the house from the unruly sun in the summer. In winter, the structure radiated confidence from the sun's welcome rays, and the glow of prosperity emanated throughout the rooms. Our farmlands expanded amid the flowering hawthorn bushes and cascades of fresh leaves blended in their greenery. It became apparent to everyone in Ipswich that Father had become one of the larger landowners.

Mother's spirits improved as she tasked herself with the purchase of new furniture pieces for the added space in our home. The handsomely constructed oak cabinet dressed with pewter and latten ware was the jewelry of our great new hall. Mother added to the collection each week while Father ordered shelves to enshrine the cupboard so the flourishing collection could be displayed.

Mother was in an unusually good mood one particular day as she bolted through the front door and saw Father resting on his favorite chair near the hearth. "Richard, there you are. I have a plan to make our home the most fashionable in all of Ipswich."

"What news have you heard from the lovely ladies of Boston now, my dear?" chuckled Father with a mocking tone. Father knew all about gossip.

"You must listen. Mistress Arnold just returned from her sister's home near Boston, and they are painting the walls inside and out with a salmon color. That color would look grand on the outside of this house."

Knowing the conventions in Ipswich, Father wouldn't think of it. He had no desire to be paid a visit from the authorities about the color of our home. He and Mother had been summoned to court before when Mother wore a silk scarf, which back then you had to be worth £200 to wear. He showed the magistrate their records and no more was said of it. "The walls of our home will remain white like every other home in Ipswich," Father pronounced.

Father also had no desire to get caught up in the fray of jealousy that pervaded Ipswich. A good many of the townswomen and men would take sides against their neighbors. They would harbor resentment that perked up when they needed to settle a new dispute. Someone would accuse a neighbor of taking up hay from their fields and then take him to court with an army of witnesses.

Father had been accused a number of times, most notably by Tom Wells. "Curse that man," he said, reliving the memory as he so often did. "I told him I had more work than I could handle, but he pleaded with me to write that lease contract for his farm. And then he claimed I cheated him because I reaped such a fine profit. He didn't even acknowledge that I had to hire extra men to bring in his harvest along with my own."

Father had always been shrewd, using the gossip of the town to his advantage. Most men didn't tolerate the chin-wag of the goodwives; they would find a compelling reason to leave when their chattering began, but Father would sit quietly within earshot of the discussion. Mother also reported opportunities she had overheard, so Father stood ready to make an offer when a landowner was in distress.

Being the second son in his family, Father had inherited no land. Mother always said he must have charmed his way onto the ship in Suffolk as he had little money save the meager inheritance meant to purchase land in this new colony.

Wells, stricken with gout, claimed Father took advantage of his inability to read the papers and led him to sign documents to which he did not agree, adding dates and lowering the lease price.

"I assure you, everyone in that courtroom knew Thomas Wells was a liar and a fool!" Father said. Wells brought two witnesses, neither of whom had been present at the time of the contract. Father presented himself with an air of confidence and respectfully pled not guilty. He assured the court that Goodman Wells was quite clear of mind during the agreement and that he was now disgruntled because Father had gained a bountiful harvest of corn, hay, and rye, more than had ever been grown on that very lot.

Father left the court deemed as a righteous man, but Thomas Wells and his cohorts undoubtedly lay in wait to seek revenge upon our family when the time was ripe.

Father now walked over to the Bible stand. "It is always the same group against another in Ipswich. It goes on like this with contempt lying dormant only to be resurrected with the same fury as before. Enough of this now. It is time for our Scripture reading."

With the problems of jealousy came growing beliefs of unnatural activities and pacts with the Devil. The townsfolk scoured their souls and those of their neighbors for even the faintest of stains. Satan surely had been roaring in Ipswich and threatened to become unchained.

# CHAPTER SIX

The next summer held little grace for me with John Beare in my life. John was Father's partner in prosperity while I became about as important as the family's favorite heifer. My only contribution to the household was searching for suitable herbs for Mother's poultices and medicines.

The warm days brought a mountain of chores for everyone on the farm—from milking cows to harvesting hay and planting crops. John worked with our servants in the fields while Father and Peter built new fences around our newly acquired lands. Mother oversaw the servants as they weeded and carried water for her gardens. My lone task was to visit the cool forests each day and bundle herbs to suspend from the rafters in the garret. Only I seemed to notice their pleasant aroma wafting throughout the house.

One morning in late June, when the seed was already in the ground, John stayed behind to nurse a wound on his leg from a clumsy accident while wielding the scythe. Sitting in Father's favorite chair, he rocked back and forth and gnashed his teeth.

On her way out, Mother inquired about his pain.

"The scythe cut like a knife through butter, Joan, but your cool poultice makes the pain bearable. Thank you. Last night it was like my bone was smoldering."

"Well, keep that leg up on the stool, and let the servants tend to you. I'll be off now. Our quota of spun yarn is due within a week, and Goody Kinsman has asked me to join her family while they also spin. I expect to finish my task before nightfall, but I've given Sarah instructions for your care."

Father and Mother rarely left John and me alone, and I was eager to ask about his new friendship with the Downing brothers. I had spied the three together in the fields the previous Tuesday, likely discussing topics enjoyed only by young men.

Gathering a layer of my burgundy skirt, I sauntered into the room with only pleasant intentions. "John, would you wish for a cup of tea? Mother made a pot from strawberry leaves. She says this tea has great value in calming pain."

John's silence wasn't about to deter me. I walked to the kitchen hearth to pour two cups. Through the window, I could see the servants enjoying their midday meal under a shady oak. The cups rattled as I walked into the main room.

"I saw you and the Downing brothers with some other young men out in the fields and at the village green. Are you finding their acquaintance a good way to improve Father's lands?"

"Such things are none of your concern, Mehitabel. Don't pretend to have an interest in men's business."

"I just wonder what kinds of issues young men discuss. Someday I may need to consult my husband about such affairs."

"Ah, all you know how to do is show your prettiness and silks and waste your time in the woods looking for worthless roots and leaves." John's voice was filled with disdain.

"John Beare, you are ignorant. Mother has been careful to teach me about the valuable herbs that are secret knowledge to most others. I do her a great service by bringing her the choicest ones."

"Mehitabel, you are a most foolish and ignorant girl. Your mother sends you to the forest so she can see you less and less. The happiest moments of her day are when you are away."

At that moment, I hated John more than ever, and I realized he must hold like feelings about me. My passions raged, and I lashed out. "John, why do you hate me so?"

"Mehitabel, I don't hate you," John Beare retorted, with a self-righteous grin. "Hate is a great sin. I simply see you as a foolish girl who is a curse to her father. My own mother said you were. She said you weren't worthy to be in this family." John turned away as if to dismiss me from his presence and then uttered under his breath, "Bastard of a serving girl."

My body quivered with what threatened to be an explosion of tears. The bite of John's wickedness was overwhelming, and I burst into a fury of words. "John Beare, I have hated you since the moment you came into this house!"

My hands clenched together over my lips so I wouldn't utter another word. I scurried to my room and lay on my bed, pondering what John had just alleged. Mother made no pretense of ever trying to be a real mother to me. Others mocked me just as John did, always when no one else could overhear. I knew nothing of my birth mother; I was indeed a bastard.

I was truly alone in the world, save for Father, but he was preoccupied with the rapid prosperity that had come to our family since John Beare's arrival.

I shielded myself with my warm coverlet. Could it be true that Mother only put on a mask of excitement when I came home after hours of choosing what I thought to be choice treasures? Oh, how I wanted things to be as they once were—before John came into our lives.

I contemplated ways to force John to leave our home. I knew I couldn't change Father's view of him as the adopted son for whom he had longed. And Mother tolerated him because her lot in life had improved with more possessions and servants to manage.

Could I use some of the poisons from the woods I had been cautioned to avoid? No, that plan would be foolhardy. My skill in physick was becoming well-known, and I would be suspect.

And then, my breath caught in my throat as I recalled the shame brought to a few of our townsfolk because of some young men's unrestrained passions. John just admitted he thought I was pretty. It would be natural for him to try to pursue me in an unchaste manner while both Mother and Father were away. Father would surely be enraged when John's actions came to light.

# CHAPTER SEVEN

My mind reeled with a tempest of words as I hastily constructed a story to tell Father. I scurried down the stairs with my burgundy cape, knowing my story would make no sense if I remained in the house with John Beare. Edward, our young servant, abruptly opened the door and hit me in the head. His eyes widened when he saw the panic on my face; he likely feared he was in much trouble.

I staggered to the front post and frantically considered my choices. Then I ran to the barn and climbed up on the hay, where I would stay until Father came home. The hogs squealed, and the hens moseyed in and out of the barn while I rehearsed my story and waited for time to pass.

As dusk began to settle, I made my way quietly to the front entrance to listen for Father's return. At the first sound of the horses' hoofbeats, I ran back and fell upon the hay to lie with my favorite horse and wait for Father to search for me before total darkness descended.

Finally, he opened the door and led the horses into the dimly lit barn. "Time to put you down to rest after the day we've all had," he murmured. "I'm weary, too, my friends."

I commenced a litany of soft sobs, just audible enough to attract Father's attention.

"Who goes here?" he asked in a startled voice.

I exaggerated my cries just a bit and decided it was time to launch my charade. "Father! Is that you?"

Father followed the direction of my voice and found me curled up on the hay near Destiny. "Dear child, why are you here and not in the house safe with John Beare and the servants? They could not tell me where you were."

I rushed into his arms, with tremors traveling through my body. "Father, I never expected John to consider doing such a shameful thing. He is such a wicked young man!"

"Mehitabel, dear one. What are you telling me? What is causing you to tremble?"

"Father, I was taking pity upon John because of his injury, and I asked if he would like a cup of tea and a freshly made poultice. As I came near to give him the sack, he leaped from his chair and grabbed me and would not let me go."

I buried my distressed, teary face into Father's jacket. "He … he began to touch me in wicked areas on my body and pushed me to the floor. I got away by kicking him on his injured leg, and I then crawled to the door. I was shaken and ran to the barn so John would not find me. I've been hiding in the hay."

Father cradled me in his arms for a moment. Then he put one hand on my shoulder and the other under my chin. "Mehitabel, is there more you should tell me about what John did?"

"No, Father, I managed to escape before he could truly hurt me."

Father wrapped his arms around me as he had done many times before and said, "For God's protection, I am grateful." With his arms still around me, he kissed my forehead and led me from the barn with his lantern; the house was now enveloped in complete darkness. Before we entered, Father said, "Go directly to your room and remain there while I speak with John." I was relieved I would not have to be present when Father confronted John. My plan was working so well.

"John! Where is John!" Father bellowed as he entered the door. Both Mother and John were startled when they saw Father's countenance. His face was uncharacteristically solemn and Indian red. His breaths were so deep they could be heard across the room. "Go to your room and rest, Mehitabel," he said, and then words of angry chastisement exploded from his mouth.

"John Beare, I have treated you better than a son, and yet you bring disrespect to this home and shame to my own blood! Your punishment will come from the wrath of my own hands. Then you will be sent to the jailer this night for what you have done to Mehitabel!"

Mother sprang from her chair and placed herself behind Father. I lingered at the top of the staircase to observe Father's fury and John's exile from our lives. Mother glanced up at me and studied my face. I moved out of her sight and sat on the top step to catch a glimpse when she was not looking.

"Uncle, honestly, I have been sitting on this chair near the entire afternoon, nursing my wounds and reading from the Psalms to calm my pain. Who has uttered false witness against me?" John's words brought a shiver to my soul as his tone appeared sincere and innocent. "Uncle, from whom have you heard?"

Father's rage increased as he spoke. "I found Mehitabel hiding in the hay, with her entire body trembling in terror of what you had done to her in our absence. I've been a fool to think I could leave a young man who possesses such evil motives with a young innocent. I should have had the servants attend to her while we were gone. No, I should never have allowed you into my house."

"Uncle, the servants have been diligently about with their chores and have been caring for my needs in your absence. Peter and Hugh have consulted me on their instructions so frequently that they were a distraction to my meditations. Sarah and Hannah have been nearby in the kitchen constantly attending to their chores. See the sumptuous meal they have prepared?"

"Mehitabel told me she attempted to tend to your wound and sought to bring you a comforting poultice when you made a vile attack upon her."

"Sir, that is blatantly untrue!" John's voice now equaled the rage of my father's. "The servants have been my constant witnesses these many hours and can attest to my innocence."

Father was not persuaded and drew in a deep breath to contain his anger.

Mother again glanced back to see if I was still in view and then broke in their heated words. "Richard, how did Mehitabel break free from such a strong young man as John? Surely, the servants would have heard her screams and come to her aid if they were nearby." Mother's voice was calm and steady as she began to see through contradictions I had not considered.

"Joan, Mehitabel was trembling in the hay and hidden from view as I entered the barn to settle the horses. She told me John attacked her and meant her great harm, but she kicked him violently on his injured leg to force him to break his grasp upon her. She was wise to get away by the only way she knew." Father's tone softened, and his eyes darted from Joan to John in confusion. I could hear my story unravel.

Mother's demeanor grew even more calculated as she approached John. "Let us see your injury, John, and then we can determine how forcefully Mehitabel fought off your vile actions."

John stumbled to the bench and unwrapped the cloth that held the sack of poultice. Mother knelt at his side and examined the wound.

"Richard, John's injury is healing well. I wrapped his bandage myself this morning and gave him several potent herbs to heal the gash. I left a supply of healing teas and gave Sarah instructions on how to assist him. I never spoke to Mehitabel about how she could help John."

I should have escaped to my room and closed the door to gain composure, because I now needed a new solution to counter my reported missteps.

Mother did not wait for Father to seek me out. Before I could move, she climbed to the top of the stairs and dragged me by the arm into Father's presence. "Richard, John's injury has much improved in the hours we were gone. I see no indication of new injuries as there would be if Mehitabel's story were true."

Father recoiled at this news, and his shoulders lowered to consider her words. "Mehitabel, come in front of everyone so we can try to uncover if lies have been told."

Mother's words emboldened John's quick mind. "Uncle, please fetch all the servants—Hugh, Peter, Hannah, Sarah, and also young Edward—who have been about the house all day."

Father's shouts to the servants brought them scurrying into the main rooms from the kitchens and their small rooms within the lean-to. They stood in a straight line with young Edward cowering behind the others.

"Tell me, each of you, what you witnessed inside this home while I was away."

Hugh spoke first. "Sir, I have been busier than usual, tending to the chickens and keeping the hogs from the tender corn. Peter and I spent much time repairing the fences as the hogs had torn through the main gate in the fields near the creek. When we returned to the house, we observed Sarah and Hannah tending to the pottage and stews, and they began the baking of bread for your return. That is all, sir."

Peter studied our faces and began his testimony. "Sir, I beg your pardon, but from the kitchens just now we overheard the words said about Mehitabel and John. I witnessed no commotion, but young Edward needs to tell you what he overheard after our midday meal, which we ate outside." Peter spoke with authority and shook his head, looking in my direction. "Edward, come forward. You must tell our good master what you told us in the fields."

Edward peeked from behind Sarah's skirts. Hugh grabbed him by the corner of his shirt and pushed him forward to stand directly in front of Father.

"Edward, speak about what you heard, or I shall beat it out of you," said Father, with unusual harshness.

Edward's entire body cringed as he wiped the tears streaming down his cheeks. "Sir, I was placing wood near the fireplace in the kitchen as I do many times each day when I heard Mehitabel shouting at John. I saw nothing and heard little said between them. Mehitabel then went to her room for a long while and later came down the stairs so quietly a shaft of straw could be heard. She went out the door as quickly as she could with her shoes and cape in her hand."

A silence settled over the room, and Father waited for the revelation of more evidence. Mother clearly could contain herself no longer.

"Richard, I am beginning to see the truth here." She bent down in front of young Edward, and with a kind, motherly manner put her hand on his shoulder. "Edward, is there any more you could tell us? What words did you hear? There will be no beating or trouble if you answer with God's honest truth."

"Mistress, I heard John say his mother told him that Mehitabel was a curse to you and the master. Then Mehitabel shouted that she hated John and wanted him out of this house. From a distance, Peter saw Mehitabel walk with much haste to the barn."

Hannah broke in, "Mistress, Edward reported to us that he observed Mehitabel with her red cape on as she headed to the barn, and she was looking back and forth to see if anyone had spotted her. We were certain Mehitabel had concocted some evil deceit and wanted no witnesses."

Hugh, who had been mostly silent up to now, finally spoke. "Sir, we found it odd that Mehitabel had left the house not to be seen by anyone for many hours. This is most strange since she asks us to wait upon her needs many times each day. Often, she asks us to accompany her to the village green so she can spy on the young men of the village."

Father sank into his chair and put his hand under his chin; his silence was agonizing. When he finally spoke, it seemed to seal my fate. Calling each servant by name, he said, "Would you put your hand upon God's Word to swear to the truth of your words about Mehitabel? Has John honestly been sitting in innocence the afternoon?"

Each servant offered to swear upon the Bible that my story was false. Father dismissed them to their rooms.

Mother wasted no time. "Richard, Mehitabel has once again made you the fool. This story will soon be carried to the villagers, mark my word! It is time for your daughter to be sent out to a neighbor's home. It won't be too many years for her to be married. Who would want such an unruly wife, the way she is now?"

"Enough, Joan. It is clear that Mehitabel told a lie, but perhaps there is a reason, or perhaps there is more to her story."

"Richard, you have always been blind to your daughter's lies and laziness. She is like Eli's sons in the Old Testament. Think what our minister will say when he finds out about Mehitabel's lies—and you know he will! It will be *you* he chastises!"

The disappointment in Father's eyes pierced my heart. "Mehitabel, why did you lie about John? He has been such a hard worker since he arrived and is like a son to me."

*Like a son to me*, echoed in my ears. My heart sank. I couldn't counter the compelling testimony of our servants on John's behalf. "I don't know why I did it," I sobbed, the words choking through my tears.

How I wished this day could be erased from my life! The person I sought to destroy had emerged triumphant. And my life of privilege could change forever.

# Chapter Eight

Banished to my room, I sat alone with only Sarah to bring me food and tend to my most basic needs. Sabbath services were my only respite. I attended each Sunday in a futile effort to keep the story of my devious scheme from spreading throughout Ipswich. Mother spoke not a word to me when we entered the meetinghouse, and I sat in holy terror of the further shame I might bring upon our family. Richard Braybrooke's sixteen-year-old daughter was virtuous no more, and Ipswich's women and men now mocked me with their whispers. During services, a hushed silence paired with their disapproving eyes.

Each day seemed like eternity's darkest night. I wanted all the pain erased as if the past three months never happened. Father walked about the village in uncharacteristic somberness as my tattered tale lay scattered about the village and magnified beyond what I could ever imagine. In the eyes of the village women, Mother's gossipy stories of my past sixteen years were vindicated. In our home, her screams caused the very beams to rattle as she asserted I was "the Braybrooke curse" or more frequently "the bastard child." Father could no longer defend me.

My place in the family was lower than the servants: I had no discernable purpose and was one who should be discarded. My actions and words deserved no pity or tolerance, but I clung to the hope that time would bring forgiveness.

I studied the apple trees at a distance from my window. *How things change in just a few months.* Just a couple of weeks back they were a wiry tangle of last season's growth, a mess of unruly twigs and overgrown branches. Now they held the promise of new life and fruitfulness. Perhaps Mother might allow me to go to the woods once again to look for herbs. Quiet as a mouse with a secret, I tiptoed down the creaky wooden stairs. Before I reached the middle landing, I heard John Beare and Mother's voices. I pressed my back against the wall to remain undetected.

"Don't you be concerned about your uncle. I know he still intends to give you that land in Wenham when you are of age. Don't you worry," said Mother.

"But, Joan. He now treats me with indifference, not like it was before. I should have never told him about how Mehitabel had attempted to seduce me—and on more than one occasion!"

*Me? Seduce John Beare! What a bold-faced lie!* I stood frozen against the wall, not able to scream in my defense.

"Johnny, Richard has heard tales of how coy and flirtatious Mehitabel can be with the young men in the village. The neighbors have been only too quick to tell me how Mehitabel displays herself in provocative ways at the village green and sometimes even in the fields."

*Those old biddies! Obviously jealous of my silks and pretty face.* Exaggerated though they were, I could not defend myself against those accusations.

It was true that many of the young men had viewed me as a suitable or even desirable wife, due to my father's increasing wealth. My physical beauty surpassed most of the other girls in the village since my face remained unblemished. How fortunate I had been; now I was transformed into an unchaste and sinful creature. The people of Ipswich believed John's truth rather than my lie; that he was in no condition to pursue me; that I used his weakness as an opportunity to banish him from the family. There would be banishment, but not of John.

One Sunday in early May, Reverend Hubbard approached my father before services. It was no surprise my wicked deeds had reached the ears of God's representatives here on Earth. He asked Father to consider a suitable solution to our family's situation. Always obedient to our minister, Father asked Reverend Hubbard and his wife to be guests in our home for the afternoon meal.

During the service that morning, I studied Reverend Hubbard with great intent since I knew he held my fate in his hand. William Hubbard was a learned man who graduated from Harvard and spent most of his time writing and preparing his sermons. He was unlike the other ministers who shared the pulpit at our services. Most employed an angry and fervent tone when they spoke about God's condemnation of sinners. Reverend Hubbard's voice rose with authority and passion as if our eternal destiny was in his hands. He would lean forward with his hands firmly on the lectern as he admonished us with strong words of conviction, but then his voice would soften, and he would remind us of God's love for His children. He always spoke with genuine affection for his congregation, and I prayed that his kindness and mercy would be evident in the coming discussion.

I heard the polite voices of both Reverend and Mistress Hubbard as they entered our home after the morning church gathering. Father and Mother turned off their rough behaviors and manners and switched to a more genteel disposition, with carefully chosen words, as they usually did when conversing with the more elite in Ipswich. Their voices trailed off as they all moved to the hall to discuss my fate.

Perched at the top of the staircase, struggling to overhear the conversation, I sprang up as Sarah rounded the corner from the kitchen and ascended the steps with my meal. "You should take care to enjoy this fine meal as it may be the last you will ever be served in this house or likely any house." She set my food directly on the stairs, spilling part of the stew on the top step. "You might want to learn to clean that up since you may be doing a lot of that in your days to come."

Sarah scampered quickly down the stairs, perhaps in fear I might tell Father about her impertinence. Her words ate at my gut. She had been privy to the conversation downstairs while serving the guests.

I crept down the steps a bit further to hear the discussion. Father made an attempt to convince the Hubbards that a more suitable placement should be found, considering our family's elevated station in Ipswich. I heard Father's desperation. "Yes, Reverend. I can see Mistress Hubbard has a suitable plan for Mehitabel, but I ask that you consider she be placed as a dutiful servant in your household instead of with neighbors of such low station. Certainly, she admires you both and for so many years has spoken with gratitude of your kindness."

Reverend Hubbard's tone indicated the matter was settled. "Richard, Joan. Margaret and I made numerous discreet inquiries; I assure you. The Chipmans are the only ones who will consider taking Mehitabel. I also assure you they promised not to make her duties too severe, but they do expect payment in exchange for their leniency."

Mistress Hubbard added, "Goodman Braybrooke, I give you our word we will make efforts to see that Mehitabel is well treated, but she must understand her reputation in Ipswich will not soon be forgotten. I have watched her for many years, and I know she will be greatly repentant and will make every effort to win herself back into your home."

The Hubbards stood to depart. "Richard, we will bring our carriage to your home after services before sundown to deliver Mehitabel to her new home." With that parting instruction, Reverend Hubbard made his way back to the church for the afternoon meeting, and Father went outside to speak to the servants.

I collapsed into a heap like dirty rags in the corner of the hallway, hearing how my fate was sealed. The next words heard were Mother's, but to whom she spoke I knew not. "Perhaps our curse will be broken from this day forward. I will be most fortunate never to glance upon Mehitabel's lying mouth again."

# CHAPTER NINE

My heart wept. The only people I loved and admired had abandoned me. My tale of deceit, so impervious to reality, had sealed my destiny. A man of God such as Reverend Hubbard would never allow a creature like me as a servant in his home.

I had always expected these years to be filled with instruction in the ways of a godly wife. My status now tumbled into that of a serving girl, for which I was ill-equipped. Never to be fully trusted, I would forever be scrutinized as a lowly hawk follows its prey.

My mind was left scorched from the remains of the fire ignited by my foolish words. My silk coverlet enveloped me for perhaps the last time. As I lay in bed that night, my hope was, as Mistress Hubbard had said, that I might someday return and find comfort in this lonely room again.

Father had barely spoken to me since that fateful day of my tale. I had shattered his heart and proved Mother to be the wiser judge of my character. In her eyes, I was more rebellious and troublesome than the unruly sea. And her opinion of me was vindicated; that was the cruelest thought of all.

Sure to his word, Reverend Hubbard arrived alone that afternoon. I was relieved, as I could not bear to see the disappointment on Mistress Hubbard's loving face. She had been nothing but kindhearted to me, and I made her steadfast confidence in me now seem foolish.

Father came to my room, leaving Reverend Hubbard in the company of Mother, who made a great pretense to appear saddened by my departure. Mother always put on a veil of propriety and kindness when in the company of the Hubbards. The Reverend was too wise a man not to see beyond her feigned expressions of grief.

Father sat on the small stool near my bed. "Mehitabel, I know we have not discussed that you would leave this house until now, but Mother and I have agreed this arrangement is best. Child, know my heart breaks, but our good minister has found an agreeable family in Topsfield for you to live with, for just a while."

Father's words did not reveal the truth his heart must be suffering. "You will be sent out to Josiah Chipman and his wife, good people who have need of a young woman to help with the children. Goody Chipman is ill in bed, suffering from her recent travail. She is still running a fever, and her newborn infant needs much care. You have learned many remedies that could bring healing and will be of great help to them."

Father started to put his arms around me but instead patted my shoulders as if afraid to touch me. He quickly removed his hands and gave me a bag for my clothing.

"Mehitabel, you must know that I do this out of love for the hope of your restoration and to give Mother time to ..." There was a long silence. "For Mother to also repent of her sins against you. I regret I have been a too-tolerant husband, and I know you have suffered in great silence because of it. Try to pray for forgiveness for your sins and those committed against you. Mother and I also need to beg and pray for forgiveness. I shall try to help her see this is so."

With Father's slightly comforting words, I placed a few of my worldly belongings into the woolen bag. As a servant, I would have no need of fine silks or laces or my well-made skirts or capes. I chose only what was prudent and necessary for my new life.

The ride to Topsfield was long, with a great wall of silence between Reverend Hubbard and me. He finally broke the stillness by asking me to recite the Scripture verses I held in my memory. I stumbled through a great many, and the icy partition between us began to melt.

Reverend Hubbard was a kind man with twinkling eyes, full of sincerity and wisdom. "Mehitabel, I recall many of those verses were the exact ones you learned at the knee of my good wife. Those were excellent times, were they not? It warms my heart as your minister to know words of Scripture are embedded in your heart."

The horse's steady trot against the dry ground calmed my mind. The even rhythm distracted me as I recalled happier times for just a moment. "Yes, Reverend, I owe much gratitude to you and Mistress Hubbard. The two of you and Father are the people always closest to my heart."

Reverend Hubbard slowed the carriage. He pulled the horse to a complete stop and then turned to me. "Mehitabel, you made no mention of your mother. As your minister, I ask that you tell me what prevents your heart from giving worthy tribute to one who has raised you."

I thought for a moment of my error in not mentioning Mother. As always, my heart was bursting to tell someone what I had endured these sixteen years. "Reverend, Mother told me that I brought a curse to her the day I was born. I have known for many years that she is not my true one and that my birth mother was a whore. I have not been told of how this came to be. I only know Mother has been forced to pretend, to act like my mother to the world. Her contempt is all I have ever known. I have endured it every moment of my life."

If it had been proper, I believe Reverend Hubbard would have wished to comfort me, but instead, he gave a short tap to the reins, and we were off at a faster pace than before.

The glowing sun in the west joined the line where heaven touched the earth. "We will soon be at the Chipmans' home, Mehitabel," Reverend Hubbard said as the cart rounded the bend. "I must tell you before we part ways. Mistress Hubbard and I have a thorough knowledge of your father and mother's past, but we must let God be the one who seeks vengeance. You must not try to ask or think about it. I only wish your father had asserted his responsibilities in a manner more fitting for a Christian man and husband."

"But my father is innocent. He has always been loving toward me."

"Your father loves you, that is true, but your mother's shame has been poisoned by a hard heart and an evil tongue. The Lord will not forgive her until she seeks full repentance for the sins committed against you. You are an innocent child, not a curse. Hold God's Holy words close to your heart. Fast and pray and ask for God's forgiveness for your sins, and He will bring you to full repentance." Reverend Hubbard added, "Know that you will be in our daily prayers, Mehitabel."

The flood of God's love washed over me, but as I turned to look at my new home, the harsh reality of my situation took over.

There stood Josiah Chipman at the entrance with his legs planted out wide and a sheen of sweat covering his face. Four of his children—three boys and a girl, all under the age of seven—were running about the garden, which was rife with overgrown weeds.

Reverend Hubbard assisted me with my bag as I stepped off his cart. "Josiah, this is Mehitabel, who is eager to be of assistance to your family. She carries some of her mother's healing herbs for your wife."

Goodman Chipman shook the minister's hand and then glared at me from head to toe.

"Josiah, I must depart before the roads flood with night terrors. Goodbye, Mehitabel. I am confident you will be a blessing here."

I clutched my bag as tears ran down my cheeks. Josiah then summoned his children to meet me. There they stood with mischievous grins, swinging their arms back and forth in a manner that was almost defiant.

"This is Elizabeth," he said, motioning to the girl. "She has been helping her mother until now. She will tell you what to do." Josiah turned and walked away. I gave out a heavy sigh, and except for Elizabeth, all the younger ones scattered.

"You will sleep next to the fireplace in a sack stored in the old pine bench," said Elizabeth as she stared at me. "Father said that I must try to help but only to explain your duties and chores in our household. You must do all the cooking and care for my brothers, but I am to take care of the baby, not you. We have not had a meal since early morn, and Father said you would prepare dinner when you arrived."

I became the only servant to a household with sickness, a baby, and four impertinent children. Two-year-old Luke was forever helping himself to the bread left on the table to cool, and Samuel had no fear of the wild animals who felt invited into the house with the door constantly left open. I encountered one challenge after another and collapsed in my bed sack each night.

Surely, our servants at home had all the responsibilities I bore, but there were no young children or a sick woman for whom to care. I had no time to venture into the woods for medicines, not that I would want to with Elizabeth's warning of a forest fraught with Indians, waiting for me to come in deep so they could carry me off.

I found little time to pray except at Sunday meetings, and even then it was almost impossible since I was expected to keep the young ones on the bench with me at the meetinghouse in Topsfield. The intense summer heat induced the children to fuss, talk, or whine while the minister droned on. The hard tap on their heads from the tithingman's stick had little effect. Their father cast disapproving looks our way, but the stony glare directed at me was most eerie. Josiah's gaze was not one of disapproval but a strange lewdness both unwelcome and repulsive.

As Mary Chipman gained strength, she scrutinized me as I moved about during my chores, taking care never to allow her husband to be alone with me. Neighbors often came to spend the day, and I could hear them whispering about the scurrilous tales of my past. As her health improved, Mary was urged by Josiah to go for an occasional walk to sit with a neighbor and help with the spinning in return for the many favors and tasks they had provided during her illness. She always cautioned Elizabeth never to let me out of her sight.

In mid-June, Goody Chipman was summoned to her sister's home in a nearby village. She gave no reason, but the satchel of healing herbs she placed in her basket made me suspect someone was ill. She glared at me with suspicion as she turned to leave. Her shrill voice punctuated her sharp, commanding words as she delivered a hill of instructions, wagging her finger at me all the while. "Mehitabel, I am now leaving, but I could return at any moment, so don't laze around. Remember that the lye and fat are already in the kettle outside, so don't forget to tend to that chore also. The soap is ready only when the mix becomes thick and frothy."

I set about my arduous chores inside the house while trying to remember that I also needed to stir down the lye and fats in the outside kettle. Since no one was inside, I rested my head on the table next to the bowl of peas for just a short respite from the drudgery.

"Mehitabel! My hand!" Seth rushed into the house screaming, his right hand covered with a fiery bubble.

"Oh, Seth, what did you do?" I grabbed a wet cloth and rushed to his side to cover his hand.

"I was trying to stir the soap in the kettle," he replied with tears streaming down his cheeks. "I was just trying to help you. I stood on a bucket, but the kettle tilted and burned my hand."

"Oh, Seth, you wanted to help. Always so inquisitive and adventurous. Let me try to find an herb in the woods for this burn. We must bring back your cheerful smile. Elizabeth, stay with Seth while I search for witch hazel near the edges of the forest."

I was close to the tree line when I noted Josiah working in the nearby cornfields. I waved my hands above my head to get his attention for help and frantically pointed toward the woods so he might keep watch for Indians. Hopefully, he would understand I was going into the woods, even if he didn't know the reason.

I scurried from tree to tree, searching for plants to soothe Seth's burn. Suddenly I heard loud footsteps from behind. My heart raced with the thought of savages. I turned, and there was Josiah running through the trees. He ran up to me, his eyes ablaze, and grabbed me by my waist, pushing me onto a bed of leafy plants. I kicked and screamed, digging my shoes into the ground to get away. He slapped me across the face to stop my shrieking and then began to tear clumsily at my waistcoat.

I heard Elizabeth's cries from a distance: "Mehitabel, do you see Indians?"

Elizabeth's voice was getting closer as she ran toward me. She stopped in horror when she saw me struggling with Josiah. Elizabeth's trembling hands covered her face, and she ran back toward the house—and was greeted by her mother who had just returned.

The sweat from Josiah's forehead dripped into my eyes, but I continued to kick at him with my feet. The sound of Goody Chipman's screams jolted him, and he darted into the forest. I clung to the safety of a nearby tree, wiping his sweat from my brow. I emerged from the forest with no cap and a dirtied and ripped skirt and bodice, grateful for getting away. I couldn't believe I was now safe, but there stood Goody Chipman, her face ablaze with fury, and young Elizabeth at her side.

"Mother, I rushed to see because I heard screams in the woods. I think Father was with Mehitabel," Elizabeth reported.

Goody Chipman lunged forward and slapped and punched me, pulling my hair so brutally that a large clump ripped from my head. She stormed back to her home and returned moments later with my few possessions and hurled them at my head.

"Whore! I'll not have some whoring servant girl in my home! Ingrate! This is the thank-you I receive for taking you off your mother's hands? Get off with you!" screamed Goody Chipman.

My head was spinning and bleeding. I had nowhere to turn. I walked to the local minister's home to tell him my story. The minister and his wife just shook their heads. He led me to the barn, and his wife returned in a few moments with a small blanket and a wet cloth for my head wound.

My future was more dismal than I could ever have imagined. I tried to explain the series of events to the minister the next morning, but his stone face showed he did not believe me. He loaded me into the cart as if I were hay to be delivered and drove me back to the Hubbards' home. Like a pile of dirty rags, I sat on the doorstep while the two men of God exchanged a few remarks. His scandalous words burned through my heart.

Mistress Hubbard led me to the kitchen to tend to my wounds and filth.

"Oh, child, what has happened?" she asked.

After my retelling, she could only say, "Your story is not at all what was relayed to us, Mehitabel. I will be sure to tell this to my husband."

I knew Mistress Hubbard wanted to believe my story, but my life this past year had whittled away everyone's trust and faith. With her usual polite tone, she asked her serving girl to give me food and drink, and I was then allowed to rest in the servants' room.

My heart flickered with a hint of optimism at the thought of a position in the Hubbards' household.

The next morning a servant informed me that Reverend Hubbard requested I meet with him in his study, the one room I had never been invited to enter. She opened the door, and there sat my minister with rows of grand looking books behind him on a shelf. He didn't invite me to sit, but instead announced, "Mehitabel, Jacob Perkins and his wife have agreed to take you in as their serving girl. Your father graciously has paid a handsome fee for their goodness."

"Reverend Hubbard, please believe the story I told your wife about what happened with the Chipmans. It was *Josiah* who attacked *me* in the forest, but I know you and Mistress Hubbard must consider me such a blighted and wicked girl if you only consider the lies of the others."

"Mehitabel, you should feel fortunate. The Perkinses are godly people, already in full membership in our congregation. Their home is modest, one of the earliest in Ipswich with only two rooms. There will be only the two of them to serve, and they have no children. We will leave right after I finish my sermon notes."

I was slightly relieved to be placed in a godly house without a horde of mangy children and such a lecherous man as Josiah. I hoped and prayed that somehow I might find peace and redemption, but I had a peculiar premonition.

# CHAPTER TEN

My heart struggled with so many emotions: shame for my false accusation against John Beare, anger at Josiah's assault, and loneliness for my father. But my fears lifted when Reverend Hubbard introduced me to Jacob Perkins and his wife, Sarah.

I had known Sarah since we were young girls learning to read at the foot of Mistress Hubbard. Our esteemed minister's wife taught the young girls in her home using a hornbook and Bible while boys received their training at the Grammar School. Though Sarah was friendly, we were not true friends. Mother had cautioned me to not associate with girls who came from more humble homes, although Sarah always displayed a good heart and kind disposition. Married for just a year, she and Jacob were destined to be husband and wife since birth. I bore no fear of Jacob. He was the model of a good Puritan man who cherished his wife.

The Perkinses were my last resort. I was accepted into their home as a servant but treated with trepidation. Jacob and Sarah were careful not to include me in their private conversations and guarded their words in my presence. They were cautioned to keep our relationship as one of servant and master, and I could ask for no more. I had slipped below the status of a servant and was more like a squaw. Sarah surely must have worried I would bring unhappiness or scandal to her home. The wagging tongues of those who reviled me were always close by.

Often during those first weeks, Master Perkins traveled to the village by himself to fetch supplies while Sarah remained behind to supervise my chores. One day not long after my arrival, Sarah approached me while I prepared to scrub the stains from the table linens.

"Mehitabel, Jacob and I will be traveling to the village and will return after the heat of the day."

"Are you going for provisions?" I asked.

"Well, no. Jacob and I will be visiting with people on our trip." I suspected the purpose of their trip was to visit Reverend Hubbard and report on my progress, but it would not be appropriate for me to ask.

Jacob's face beamed as he came to gather his wife. "Ah, Sarah has likely told you of our journey. Today, we ask you to keep a watchful eye on the cornfields. My father has reported the neighbor's hogs were foraging through his crops yesterday, and they caused much destruction."

I nodded my head in agreement as Jacob continued, "I see you are already tending to the laundry we placed by the outside kettle. It's a lovely day with just a few clouds, so take time to sit in the shade to cool while we are in town. We will not expect you to make an evening meal for us." Jacob seemed merry as he and Sarah climbed into the cart.

Sarah turned to me with a smile and said, "Oh, and if there are problems, Hannah Perkins, Jacob's sister-in-law, is just a short walk from here. Mehitabel, you have been working so hard for us. A day by yourself will bring joy to your spirit."

Sarah's sweet voice brought a tinge of envy to my soul as she would be alone with her beloved Jacob. My forced smile belied my resentment, but I waved goodbye and then turned away to pout.

Perched above the outside fire, the heavy kettle was held up by a chain suspended from sturdy tree trunks pounded into the ground. The laundry task had been waiting for me since early morning. How would I ever be able to clean the table linens so heavy with grease stains? How did Father's servants rid our linens of such filth? Befuddled, I tossed the linens into the boiling water mixed with lye and stirred them with a long stick as I recalled our own servants doing. Perhaps the stains magically disappeared? I wish I had been more observant!

As I stirred, I began to think how I might never possess even stained linens such as these, nor a husband. Who would care to have such a bother of a wife? Each stir of the kettle bubbled up the despair festering in my soul. That I should envy my mistress's lowly station exposed the pitiful state of my own situation.

The sound of buzzing bees and the low croaking of frogs from the nearby pond reached my ears. One large frog with a curious brown spot like those found on the faces of the old crones in the village hopped right up to my left shoe. He jumped near the door where I had carelessly left the milk pail, enchanting me with his croak.

"Would you like a taste of the milk?" I asked as if he might answer. I uncovered the pail of fresh milk intended for the next day's early meal, then I grabbed a small branch from a nearby tree overhang and coaxed him to the pail. In he hopped, looking up to thank me for the refreshing dip in my milky pond. Sarah's morning samp would have a secret ingredient of which only I was aware. I dipped my hand into the milk, lifted Froggie out, and watched as he scurried back to the pond. A twinge of my merry spirit returned.

The sound of male voices singing floated from the nearby hay fields, and as I peered over the tall stalks of corn waving in the breeze, I could see two familiar faces—John Willyston and Timothy Bragg, whom I had not seen since my exile. John was heaving hay with a pitchfork and Timothy was tying the bales. I grabbed the pitchfork Jacob left on the side of the barn from his early morning chores and walked out to join my old friends.

"John, Timothy! Wait for me!" I shouted. They stopped their chores and rested on their tools as I sauntered across the fields.

John rocked back on his heels and sneered, "Mehitabel Braybrooke, look at you. A common serving girl now. Let me see the bumps on your hands from the hard work you now do."

I wanted John as a friend, and for him to know how my lot in life was much like his, so I overlooked his mocking tone and shared my tribulations. "My life of late has been cruel indeed. You two have little idea how evil the Perkinses are in taking advantage of my situation. But I fitted my mistress well just now. I put a frog in her milk pail." My vinegary demeanor transformed to one of smugness.

"Mehitabel, your foolishness will get you into trouble sure as we stand here. Sarah will know you are the one who did the deed," warned Timothy.

"Nay, she will never know. The frog took his morning bath in her milk just to give a better flavor and maybe some warts for her plain face!" I laughed.

John shook his head at my rudeness, and they went about their chores in quick time so their mothers would not scold them. They then bid me farewell and returned home.

For the first time in months, I had no one to keep me to task. I meandered along the stream until my hunger told me it was time to return.

The Perkins' absence gave me the desire for unbridled respite from the drudgery of my life of servitude. How pleasant it was to pretend I was the mistress of this house. Forgetting all caution, I searched the house to find the pouch of tobacco Jacob kept hidden near his gunpowder so Sarah was not privy to his vile habit. Neither Father nor Mother smoked a pipe, as it was considered a foul practice—those who desired to be elevated into the elite circles of Ipswich should never consume tobacco—but our servants had secretly shared their pipes with me, so I knew how tobacco could bring a relaxed spirit to a dismal life.

I secreted Jacob's pipe and a small snuff of tobacco and headed outside. No one was around to observe my mischief, save the chickens. The oak's branches gracing the small pond bid me come sit and enjoy the shade. Leaning against the rough bark, I stoked the small fire inside the bowl to keep the embers glowing. Drawing the smoke into my lungs gave me a curious feeling of contentment, more potent than any desire to finish my chores.

I settled my weary body under that great oak and closed my eyes to enjoy the gentle breeze. The green-tinged sunlight filtered through the clouds.

Suddenly, the squeal of hogs, or perhaps wild boars, sounded from a distance. I hurried to the outside wall of the house and climbed onto the oven where it bulged out from the broad chimney to get a better view of the fields. My bare feet slipped on the clay surface, so I set the pipe on the roof to steady myself, while clutching the dried thatch on the eaves with my other hand.

There those scoundrels were! Sure as day, stirring in the stalks were two hogs feasting on corn in Jacob's field nearby. Across the way, I could see that John Willyston had also heard the commotion. We both ran to scatter the hogs and help them find their way back to their careless owners. John knew how to entice the beasts, so our task was quickly accomplished. He carried the smallest one under his arm and bid me good-day.

As I turned back toward the Perkins' house, a sight worse than anything I could have imagined greeted me. Long, gray wisps of smoke wafted from the home, sending my heart to my feet. I ran as fast as I could, and as I approached, small flames rose from the backside of the house near the outside fireplace. The inside hearth had contained just a flicker when I was there earlier. How could the roof have erupted into such a blaze? I extinguished the flames using water from the outside kettle, leaving only a trail of residual smoke.

Relieved that there was little damage, I felt it prudent to seek out the neighbors' help as Sarah had instructed. Jacob's sister-in-law, Hannah, came to my assistance as soon as I explained that I needed help with my outside chores. I didn't want to make any mention of the fire since it was gone now and only a small strand of smoke remained. We strolled at a leisurely pace until, suddenly, we saw smoke rising above the Perkins' home. Goody Bragg and her son Timothy also came running from their fields with buckets to fetch water from the well. When we arrived, I could see that flames had erupted again in my absence.

We threw pail after pail of water onto the roof. Finally, with the fire extinguished, Hannah said, "The fire must have started in the hearth since the flames were above the oven. Let's gather whatever things we can from the house so they have no smell from the smoke." She entered first, and we all grabbed a few items that we knew would be precious to Sarah and Jacob.

Goody Bragg then clutched her son, Timothy, "Go examine the fireplaces. The fire didn't start in either of these chimneys. There are but a few brands simmering in just this one hearth, and none at all in the other."

Hannah Perkins turned to me with a scowl and pointed mockingly to the hearth where the herbs and wooden bowls stood in pristine condition. "Mehitabel! This fire clearly did not start inside. Look at the hearth. There is little stench of smoke inside!"

She reared up with her hand to slap me across the face when one of the servants shouted for us to come outside, "Fire! The thatch is on fire!"

We dashed to where a slight fire was smoldering in the dry thatch on the other side of the house, and it swiftly erupted with a huge plume. Within minutes, the entire structure was ablaze. The smoke from the fire attracted the attention of neighbors for many miles, and in no time, the whole village had arrived to douse the last flickers of flame. I sat on a stump with my head in my lap, my mind spinning in despair. How could such a tragedy have befallen my master's home? The fire under the outside kettle had long since burned out.

"Mother, come have a look at this," yelled Timothy. Goody Bragg scrambled to the back of the house. In Timothy's hand was a warm pipe with just a pinch of tobacco in it. "I found this pipe just a few steps away from the back side near the oven under the eaves. It was on the ground and is still warm. There is a slight charring on the outside of the bowl. Someone must have been having a session with this pipe."

Everyone glared at me, the assured culprit. I then remembered holding the pipe while climbing onto the oven. It must have fallen onto the thatch and smoldered there for a time before setting it on fire, and then somehow fell to the ground. I had not meant to set the house on fire, only to have a peaceful day.

The crack of the whip in the air over the horse's head signaled the arrival of the young Perkinses. Their cart came into view as it rounded past the grove of elm trees.

"Here come Jacob and Sarah!" exclaimed Hannah Perkins, scowling as she glared at me. "They will be devastated when they see their house. No paltry bag of shillings from Braybrooke is worth taking this wretch into your home!"

Goody Bragg sneered as she looked at my quivering form, "Don't expect anyone to have pity upon you, Mehitabel. Joan has been right all along!"

The villagers gathered around the cart when it came to a stop. Sarah clutched at her stomach and rocked back and forth and sobbed. Jacob's glassy stare transformed into roaring flames of rage. He staggered over to touch the few surviving remnants of his house, and his hateful glare gave the impression that he wished to ignite me.

Sarah sat on the wagon bench and continued to sob. She couldn't look at me nor could I bear to see her suffering. Jacob's brother Abraham lifted Sarah off the cart and led her to his own cart.

As he covered Sarah with a shawl, Abraham said, "Misfortune has visited you and Jacob today, but Mehitabel will soon be sent off to prison. To cause a house to burn with such wicked intent is a heinous crime."

I wanted to try to shed light on the events of the day, but the entire village was already convinced of my evil nature. Without a doubt, I was a curse to all who had me in their company.

As the constable's cart creaked up the hill on its way to the prison, I learned what it means to be a criminal. The bare wood floor and a few stalks of soiled hay were my only company. With my hands bound, I was led from the cart to the entrance of the Ipswich prison. "What is going to happen to me," I asked the constable. "How long will I be here?"

"Who knows?" the constable replied. "Likely you will languish in prison until the next court session, and after that? Maybe taken to the gallows to be hanged in a gibbet for the ravens and eagles to feed upon you." His ghoulish laugh lingered in the air as I descended the prison stairs.

# CHAPTER ELEVEN

The never-ending days dragged on in the Ipswich prison. I had seen rats and gnats before. I had been cold, hot, thirsty, and destitute; but never had these scourges been my daily companions.

Father arrived daily with a supply of fresh blankets, fruits, bread, and cheese. He sat for just a short time to provide encouragement and what little comfort he could offer. I devoured the food, surrounded by others who displayed only contempt for me.

Mother never came with Father to visit, and I could tell that our servants, not my mother, had prepared the food. When I asked about Mother, Father would reply, "Dear child, we are both heartbroken over your plight." Father was not truthful, for I had given Mother no reason to turn her heart toward me. The curse I was to her kept spreading like the weeds that threatened to strangle her precious plants and herbs. Still, I wanted to know if I would ever be allowed back in their home.

"Father, Mother is still furious with me, isn't she?" I queried. "She never visits."

"We pray for you each day, but no, Mother's feelings have not changed," said Father as his voice trailed off. "She refuses to come to the prison. Says no one in the Braybrooke family has ever set foot in jail."

Mother was correct: no one we knew could ever have described the trials I was to endure waiting for the accusation of willful arson. While the cold, filthy prison was detestable to me, the spiteful whispers all around me were the most difficult to bear. Back in Ipswich, the disapproving eyes and gossip of both the young and old crones had followed me whenever my latest foible was announced. Here, I couldn't escape their remarks or walk past them with my head held high. Their mocking words echoed off the dingy prison walls.

My fellow prisoners were familiar with the difficult life of whippings, hunger, and heavy labor. They had slept on bare dirt floors amid the scattering of vermin and animal filth. During my months as a servant, I had experienced only a few of the miseries these women had endured for a lifetime.

I knew none of them by name; Mother always instructed me not to associate with the serving class, yet I was now one of them. A few prisoners sat shackled, required to pay for this burdensome fate. I was not because Father bribed Warden Theophilus Wilson for extra privileges. My prison corner of relative luxury was due to my wealthy father who did not abandon me, but my comfort gained me few friends. Father's visits magnified the others' jealousy.

After three weeks, I feared my trial might never come. For the first time, I considered I could perish in prison. As a young girl, I had assumed I would live to a sweet old age with a dear husband much like Father and with many children blessing my years. I sank back against the cold, damp wall to ponder my fate.

High in the sky, the sun beat against the iron rails on the window over my head. The piercing light blinded me for a minute, and I shifted my covers to see. The commotion of the warden foretold that perhaps a new prisoner would be brought below. As they descended the steps, I knew by Wilson's more mannerly tone that it was more likely someone bringing food for a prisoner.

The frame of a slight woman appeared, and Wilson pointed to the corner where I sat. As she came closer, the woman struggled to find her way in the darkness. She glanced around, took in the hideous circumstances, and then softly called out my name.

"Mehitabel? Mehitabel Braybrooke, is that you I see?" I recognized this woman but did not truly know who she was. One of the many people Mother taught me to scorn, she had an aura of mystery about her. Mother would cast a piercing gaze in her direction, and the woman would look away from us as if afraid for her life. Mother would take me by the arm and drag me in the other direction. These times I recalled well, as they were the few times Mother would touch me.

I learned to be apprehensive of this woman, although no one ever told me of any hideous deeds. She must be an agent of Satan, I assumed, but no tales of diabolical acts were ever reported. Never had I been closer than twenty paces from her to study her features and to ponder how this woman could be so vile. What I now saw astonished me.

I nodded when she called out my name, although I remained frightened of her intentions. As she drew closer, I noted her beauty, though she was plainly dressed with no finery to show off her features. Her warm and comforting eyes gazed intently into mine. Yellowish locks peeking from under the brim of her coif seemed so perfect. The surrounding darkness hid the color of her eyes, but when she spoke, they twinkled just like the stars in the heavens.

"Mehitabel, I have come at the request of Reverend and Mistress Hubbard, who share my great concern for your welfare and soul. I have just a short time to spend with you. Mistress Hubbard was greatly distressed that she was not allowed to come. She sends you these foods to nourish your body and asked that I share Scripture. 'Tis nourishment for your soul."

She took my hands and held them in a reassuring embrace. My shoulders loosened, and my fears dissipated. After just a short time that I wished would not end, she released my hands and tilted my head to gaze into my face. I had an inexplicable feeling she was God's angel messenger.

"Your name is Alice, is it not? I know I have seen you many times, but we have never spoken. I'm pleased Mistress Hubbard chose you to bring me food. You are the first kind person besides Father I have seen in many weeks." My normally steady countenance quivered, and I broke out in sobs. I had not allowed myself to cry since the first day; it would have only prompted jeers and hateful comments from those around me in this foul place.

Alice sat next to me, wrapped her arms around me, and kissed my forehead. That I was vile in spirit and appearance did not seem to bother her. The smell of linsey-woolsey from her clothing was fragrant in contrast to my once finer linens, now soiled and stained. She rocked me back and forth as if I were a wee child. Her embrace filled the empty void in my soul, and my heart's desire was for this supernatural feeling to never end.

Alice moved in front of me, which was pleasing as I could better study her face and expression.

"Mehitabel, I have little time as I hear the guard pacing above us, so let me impart God's Holy Word to you. Mistress Hubbard asked that I give you God's comfort with these words from Deuteronomy: *Be strong and of a good courage, fear not, nor be afraid of them: for the Lord thy God, He it is that doth go with thee; He will not fail thee, nor forsake thee.*

Tears welled up in my eyes, and my strength seemed renewed. The verse allowed me to recall my Scripture training as a tender child sitting at the foot of Mistress Hubbard. Her gift served me well during my growing years.

"Mehitabel, you will be vindicated from these terrible troubles and vicious torments. Be strong, my child ..." Alice drew back her breath to gain composure as tears flowed from her eyes. "I have a verse for your heart, dear child." She began but then hesitated to dab her tears.

*For you formed my inward parts; you knitted me together in my mother's womb. I praise you, for I am fearfully and wonderfully made. Wonderful are your works; my soul knows it very well. My frame was not hidden from you when I was being made in secret, intricately woven in the depths of the earth. Your eyes saw my unformed substance; in your book were written, every one of them, the days that were formed for me, when as yet there was none of them.*

Wishing not to bring more tears to either of us, Alice breathed in deeply. The sense that God had just explained His mysteries and secrets was vivid. "Mehitabel, hold these words close to your heart. God will never forget you ... and neither will I."

The heavy boots magnified the thud of each step as the warden descended. "It is time."

Alice almost forgot to give me the foods from Mistress Hubbard, but we had both realized that food for my soul was needed most. She left quickly but turned back to glance at me one last time.

So many questions whirled about in my mind, but a strange silence hovered over the other prisoners. All moaning and sharp words ceased. The murmuring began again, although I could not hear anything said. Then, clear as a clap of thunder, someone whispered, "I tell you ... she has no understanding of who that woman is ... that woman, Alice."

# Chapter Twelve

Alice's visit remained a mystery. Long ago, I had asked Father to tell me what he knew about Alice. He typically diverted any conversation about unfortunates, saying it was unkind to repeat gossip. But, concerning Alice, he replied in a frightened whisper, "You must never ask about her and especially never ask Mother of her! Do you understand what I say, Mehitabel?" Father tried never to send Mother's tongue into a rage.

My spirits brightened after Alice's visit, but they were dampened the next day when Father arrived. "Mehitabel, your trial is scheduled for tomorrow morning. I will be at the meetinghouse, and perhaps Mother might also come. Please know I have done everything possible to curry favor on your behalf with the magistrates."

Father wrapped his arm around me, "I paid for the construction of a new structure for Jacob and Sarah Perkins in the hope they would be merciful during their testimony. John Beare helped secure newly made furniture for them, much better than what was lost in the fire. While I can't circumvent the law, I tried to make things right with Jacob and Sarah."

I shuddered to consider my plight. Willfully burning down a house was a capital offense, and I might hang from the gallows. "Father, I have rehearsed what I recall about that day and will speak humbly and thankfully for the goodness of the Perkinses and beg their forgiveness. Surely, with a new home, their improved lives should bring only goodwill."

"Mehitabel, it will not be so simple, and you must present yourself properly to the court officials," Father said. "Major Daniel Denison will be the chief officer to hear your case. Child, there is no one in the village who will testify on your behalf. I was not a witness and cannot testify; a father's words ring hollow and not credible. Present your actions with great remorse and innocence. The Perkinses will testify against you, but I do not know of any others. Be aware your situation is not without hope, but for a house to be set afire is a tragedy nearly as dire as a savage's attack. Choose your words carefully, my dear one."

No sleep was mine that night, and soon the rooster's crow announced the morning. It was August 15, 1668, and I awoke woefully unprepared in body, mind, and spirit to meet the challenges of my accusers, with only water for my meal.

The warden summoned me to follow him for my first court appearance. I raised my bound wrists to cover my eyes from the blinding sunlight as I climbed the stairs. Without a word, the warden led me across the road to the meetinghouse. Inside were more people than Reverend Hubbard could ever wish for on a Sunday. The esteemed and godly men and women of the village took seats behind Jacob Perkins' family, who alone numbered more than twenty-five. I approached the bench, and the warden freed my arms and hands from the shackles. I glanced warily around the meetinghouse. Father and Mother sat on the side benches next to the Hubbards, the presence of our minister giving me encouragement that the court might summon him in my defense. Alice sat far in the back, where the lowliest of servants were allowed. She nodded her head to signal assurance, giving me hope my trial would soon be over.

Seated on the lofty bench with Major Denison were Mr. Corwin and Mr. Danforth, the most recent appointments to the quarterly courts. The esteemed men towered above all others in court. Their somber expressions, framed by the white cravats about their necks, offered me no encouragement. The dark gray stone struck the solid table, and the courtroom came to order with a hushed silence. Major Denison, a tall, imposing man with a commanding and authoritative voice, sat erect as he read my accusation.

"Mehitabel Braybrooke, sixteen years of age, this court has received a complaint from Jacob and Sarah Perkins, who claim you willfully and deliberately set their house on fire with malicious intent and purpose on July 12, the year of our Lord, 1668. How do you plead to these charges?"

I lowered my head. "I swear to Almighty God I meant no harm. Sirs, I am innocent of these charges."

Major Denison's somber face did not reveal that he and the entire courtroom suspected I was guilty. Since the day of the fire, I had no friends who would give testimony to my innocence or character.

"Jacob Perkins, you are to come forward to give your sworn testimony," Major Denison declared as he crossed his arms with the stone still in his fist.

A few men gestured and shouted calls of support as Jacob walked toward the bench. Major Denison pounded with the rock to contain the crowded courtroom.

"Good sirs of the court, I can tell you the events that occurred before my wife and I left for town on the second Thursday of July. We gave Mehitabel a meager list of chores as we knew she could not be counted upon to do much without us overseeing her tasks. She was to launder linens, make hay for the animals, and be on alert for hogs in the cornfield. I milked the cows and fed the animals before we left because I feared Mehitabel would neglect the creatures. While still on our journey home in the late afternoon, Sarah and I saw smoke from a distance. We made haste in hopes of giving assistance to any neighbor who had to put out a fire in their home. As we drew closer, we saw no flames but only smoke above where my house should have been. When we arrived at what had been our home, my dear Sarah burst into tears to observe just a few of our cherished possessions sitting by the ashes. Our house burnt to the ground because of Mehitabel Braybrooke's carelessness."

When Jacob finished his accusations, Hannah Perkins, the wife of Jacob's brother, came to the stand. I had dashed to her home only for help, and now she divulged a tale that showed me to be a despicable liar.

"I should begin by telling you that Mehitabel was foolishly taken in by my husband's brother, Jacob, and his wife. Their only desire was to show God's mercy to this girl, but Mehitabel showed only a lazy and spiteful spirit in return for their kindness. Many times did Sarah come to me in tears because of problems caused by Mehitabel's willfulness. She's a liar and an unchaste creature; the whole village knows her to be so. Just consider her time with the good folks in Topsfield. Even her own mother, Joan Braybrooke, would tell you that Mehitabel has been a curse since birth."

Major Denison's voice intensified. "Goodwife, you are to tell only of the day of the fire, do you understand?"

Hannah nodded respectfully. "Mehitabel came running to our house—at least she did one thing Jacob had instructed. Said only that she needed help with the kettle of clothes she was to launder. She said nothing of a fire! I called for my servant to look after my youngest child while I tended Jacob's servant, as I am a kind woman, then I walked with Mehitabel, who was always several paces in front of me. As we walked past the large forest edge, an eerie smoke did I smell. I started running, in fear that the outside kettle had somehow sparked the nearby timber sides because of winds. But I felt no winds. I then saw the roof of Jacob and Sarah's house was sending smoke, but I couldn't yet see a fire."

Goody Perkins interrupted her testimony to wipe her brow then continued, "I called to my husband who was in the fields and signaled for him to come quickly. He was soon there with Goody Bragg and her son, who helped put out the smolders. We went inside to see what was about and to carry as many of Sarah and Jacob's furniture and precious things outside as possible. I thought there would be smoke inside the house, but there was no appearance of any smoke *or* fire. Just a few brand ends nearly dead under a small kettle hanging in the chimney. Such is how I knew that the inside fires could not have caused the roof to be on fire."

Major Denison stopped her testimony to bring clarity to her story. "Goodwife Perkins, who other than yourself and your husband saw the fire?"

"My serving boy, who followed us to Jacob's home. He came with good sense when he saw the smoke above their lands. The Braggs also."

"Have you anything else to say, Goody Perkins?"

"Aye, I do. I suspect Mehitabel brought me to Jacob's house falsely. The kettle with laundry was empty, save the linens at the bottom, when we came upon the fire. It was obvious she had already emptied the kettle to squelch a fire as we noticed a small wooden pail next to the empty pot. She must have used the pail to bail the water. She is the Devil's own spawn with her lying tongue."

With these words that pierced my heart and character, Goody Perkins took her place next to her husband, and the magistrates signaled for him to come forward and present his sworn testimony against me.

Abraham rose and with a brazen stride walked to the front. He spoke with an authority that displayed his much-practiced words. "Good sirs, I swear to God what my wife and I tell you is true. All she has said is what we were God's witness to, but I have more to say."

Abraham cleared his throat and glanced back at the crowd in the courtroom before he spoke directly to the magistrates. "Mehitabel set the fire with a pipe. Both John Willyston and I were there at Jacob's home when Mehitabel admitted she dipped up a coal from the kettle fire to light her tobacco. To add, the pipe she stole was Jacob's, and we found it still hot a short distance from the roof."

Edward Bragg, his wife Goody Bragg, and their son Timothy were the next to be called forward.

Goodman Bragg was the first to testify but hurried his words along in a stilted manner as if poorly memorized. "At my house, while I sat trying to read the Word … I would hear Goodwife Braybrooke tell my wife that Mehitabel would steal and lie, and how glad she was that Mehitabel was gone from her … that is all I have heard."

Goody Bragg shook her head in disgust and seemed resolved that her son would not be the same poorly spoken witness as her husband. She took Timothy by the arm and pinched him to begin his story.

He shuffled from side to side. His voice was muffled and faded away at the end of each sentence, but Goody Bragg coaxed each utterance out with another pinch. I had hoped Timothy would take pity on me, but my foolish words to him came back to haunt me.

"I … I was with John Willyston in the fields; just by ourselves and not bothering anyone, just doing our chores when Mehitabel came running up to us with a pitchfork in her hand. She said she wanted company making hay for the animals back at her master's home. We said hardly a word to her. Just minded our chores." Goody Bragg grabbed his elbow and pressed down hard each time his voice faded away.

"She told us, now this was before the fire, that her mistress Sarah had been angry with her that morning. Mehitabel said she had fitted her now, for she put a great toad into Sarah's kettle of milk." Timothy broke the grasp his mother had on his arm, turned, and sat down. He then stood up abruptly and said, "I swear to God," to end his testimony. Then he sat back down, and there he remained, rocking back and forth like a simpleton. I silently cursed him for repeating my folly to his wicked mother and the court.

Goody Bragg tried to hide her disappointment with her son's strange behavior but then began her part of the testimony. "Timothy wanted no part in Mehitabel's attempts to work alongside him. He'd been told about her—he knows what she is. Everyone knows. Her own mother, Goodwife Braybrooke, said to me many times in my home and hers that Mehitabel is a filthy, unchaste creature!"

Those last words resonated throughout the courtroom walls. Although I could not see Father, I knew his heart was broken and shamed. Joan, whom I always dutifully called Mother, was who the Devil chose to spread evil and gossip, using the mouths of others.

# Chapter Thirteen

All hope had vanished. It was clear no one would be summoned for my defense. The last testimony before I could proclaim my innocence was of Mary Chipman, wife of Josiah. Her husband did not possess the courage to be present in court and must have feared I might reveal the story of his lewdness against me.

With a haughty gait no godly woman should possess, Mary strutted forward and was sworn in by the magistrate. She delivered her testimony with a high-pitched screech, seemingly without ever taking a breath. "Mehitabel Braybrooke was taken in by my husband and me, but I knew from the moment she stepped off Reverend Hubbard's carriage that no good was to come from this misguided arrangement. We took her only as a great favor to our ministers, both godly men. I was ill in bed after having fevers for many days when my son Samuel was born. My dear husband could not tend to the farm and our young children. Lazy she was, and those weeks Mehitabel was with us were like a punishment from God. Mehitabel has no truth in her nor trust in her and was much given to lying and stealing. Goody Braybrooke had warned us of such."

Goody Chipman turned to me with a piercing stare. "My godly husband, if he could be here today, would tell you much more about her foul nature. The good people in this room should never be forced to hear of Mehitabel's shameful behavior. I tell you this is the truth." With another sneer, she turned and stomped back to her seat, her face beaming with great satisfaction.

My legs quivered like shriveled leaves when the magistrates summoned me forward. I walked with my head down, not daring to look at them. Surely they had already sealed my verdict.

"As others have already said, Jacob and Sarah had gone off that morning. I dared not ask any questions. They left me with not many chores and wished me a pleasant day."

Satisfied with my beginning statements giving praise to Jacob and Sarah, I then began to stumble. The previous words of testimony against me conflicted with what I thought to be true, so I stood silently. My mind was on fire with confusion, and my heart pounded so violently I wondered if others might see it beating under my jacket.

My muddled words spewed forth with little self-control. "It is true I took a pipe and sat to rest after I had done a few piles of the laundry. I then heard noises in Master Jacob's fields, so I climbed up on the oven at the back side of the house to look if there were any hogs in the corn. I placed my right hand upon the thatch of the house to steady myself. With my left arm, I accidentally knocked the pipe upon the thatch on the eaves of the house. I did not think there was any fire left in the pipe, so I gave it no more thought."

My words scattered like a flock of birds. The story I had rehearsed started to confuse me, but I stammered on. "I went down into the cornfield to drive out the hogs I saw toward the rails near Abraham Perkins' house. I looked back and saw smoke above my master's house. I was much frightened, so I went to Abraham Perkins' house to entreat Goody Perkins to help me with the kettle of clothes."

I hesitated and shook my head to reorder the story as I knew it. My practiced and guarded manner shattered, and my words sounded like those of a simple and foolish girl who was spontaneously constructing her story. "Goody Perkins and I were starting to go toward my master Jacob Perkins' house, and on the way, we saw the smoke from the house and ran. Arriving at the house, we found the fire near the place where I had knocked the pipe. I ran with a pail of water. Before I could get it out, well, the thatch flamed. For want of ladders and help, the house burned down."

Major Denison raised his hand for me to stop talking. He shook his head and began to scold me with a stern tone. "Mehitabel Braybrooke, your story makes no sense, and my mind cannot follow it. You made no mention to Goody Perkins of a fire at Jacob and Sarah's home, but instead asked her to help you launder clothes in the kettle?"

"Sir, I did not admit to Goody Perkins that there was a fire. I wanted not to frighten her."

"Mehitabel, you are indeed a foolish girl. When you first saw the fire, why did you not fully quench it? Why did you instead seek out Goody Perkins to help with laundry?"

I could no longer recall in any detail what I just gave as my sworn testimony. "I did tell Goody Perkins that the woods looked blue beyond our house, but then there was much smoke behind the house. I did quench the fire, sir. I thought the fire done. The fire in the pipe was cold, but it must have rekindled the thatch. I quenched it with lye water from the kettle."

The three magistrates now shook their heads and spoke to one another in whispers even before I ended my testimony. There was no doubt my story, so confused and muddled, would not be well received. The crowd in the courtroom shot mocking jeers as I stumbled through to finish it. There was no purpose in continuing as my fate was sealed.

The jury decided my verdict in just seconds. Mr. Corwin proclaimed, "Mehitabel Braybrooke, you have been accused and are now convicted of extreme carelessness if not willfully burning down the house. You are ordered to be whipped severely and to pay forty pounds damage to Jacob Perkins."

The warden led me down the aisle amid echoes of hoots and scoffs. "Fool! Liar! Simpleton!" the crowd shouted.

My only hope was that my foolishness and poorly chosen words of testimony had not caused me to lose the love of the four people I cherished most. I found the courage to walk down the aisle with my wrists again tightly bound but had no strength for the shame that weighed down on me like an anchor. The crushing inner voice of my disgrace followed me out of the courtroom, tormenting me with its chants: *unworthy, rejected, guilty*. Most profound was the reality that I was unlovable. The truth was clear: If you truly knew me, you would despise me. That verse was the refrain of my wretched life.

# CHAPTER FOURTEEN

How strange that returning to prison seemed the right path for me. Now I was a criminal; Mother's harsh words were true. My foolish steps in life painted me as the worst of God's creation. I didn't want to see Father's face, yet I craved his embrace. The shame of his only child's stupidity and folly must weigh heavily on his heart. Both my heavenly and earthly fathers surely had given up on me.

The familiar stench of my prison home greeted me. As I descended the stairs, only one prisoner stood to embrace me. My presence let her know the outcome of my trial.

Lydia tenderly grasped my hands and led me to my assigned place on the straw. "Here is some water for you. Tell me what happened."

"Lydia, I don't wish to relive that courtroom scene again. Please don't ask."

I couldn't stop thinking about the penalty my flesh would soon pay for my heinous deed. Although I swore not to think about it, the scene from the courtroom was recounted over and over in my mind. The pounding of the gavel and the words from Mr. Corwin: "Mehitabel Braybrooke, you are ordered to be whipped severely and to pay forty pounds …"

"Lydia, I have so much regret. Father has carried so much of my burden this past year. Just when his life seemed to be catapulting him into the upper ranks of the village …" I sighed, thankful for this cherished friend who listened to my laments again and again. "I imagine him sitting quietly at meals, with Mother nipping at his ears with gossip from the neighbors. John Beare is now his only child. There is nothing I can do to redeem myself."

Those words echoed over and over. I trembled and fell on my side into the odious straw, weeping for my past. Lydia wrapped her arms around me, using her apron to wipe my dusty tears.

"Lydia, you have shared memories of your mother, how she sang to you all day long and prayed with you at night when you were much afraid, how she put her fingers around yours as you wrote on your slate. I have no sweet memories from my mother. She could barely even tolerate my presence at meals."

Lydia nodded. "Some people are just cold and heartless, it is true."

"Mother was more than cold. I was the source of any evil or unfortunate event. In her eyes, it was I who took the place of the Devil in our home. If the stew was not to her liking, it was I who had distracted her stirring. If the cow would not give milk, it was because my curse was upon the innocent beast. I was the blame for all the disappointments in her life. My very birth cursed her womb, she would say. I was the reason she could never carry a child."

"But your father came to your defense, did he not?" asked Lydia.

"My father's love has always been true, but I've often wondered why he allowed Mother to speak to me in such a cruel way. Of course, she was most hurtful when he was not around to overhear, but she possessed a peculiar, almost eerie power over Father. Why would a man be so afraid of a woman?"

Lydia shook her head in agreement. "You are right, that is not natural. Take comfort in the thought that your ordeal will soon be over, and you will be some man's wife in not so many years."

"Oh, Lydia, far more bitter is my future. My hopes as a child were so simple. I anticipated marriage and children, to live near Father, but the crowning glories of his old age are not to be. Now the young men in the village will view me as the lowest wretch whom none would consider for marriage. I likely shall whither into an old maid, a thornback—perhaps a beggar."

Seated across from Lydia and me was an old crone who found a perverse joy in tormenting me. "Ah now, don't you weep, girl. I heard about your punishment. It is not so harsh, considering other fates you could have endured. I know many who have received much worse punishment. Neighbors whose ears were cut off or noses slit. My own brother lied to his unforgiving master about his son. For that, a hole was bored into his tongue. Pity if your mother and father had to look upon their pretty daughter with no ear or a pig snout for a nose. What husband would kiss a wife with her forked tongue?"

"Jerusha, you old fool. Hush with your stories!" Lydia chided.

"I thought Mehitabel might be comforted if she considers what could have happened. Worry not, the scars from your whipping will eventually heal," she cackled, knowing her stories would reduce me to a pool of tears.

A full two weeks passed, and not one visitor came for me, not even a message from Father, though he was still providing for me. The warden delivered my food and flipped a coin in his hand. His mocking gesture conveyed that my imprisonment was making him a wealthier man.

The faint hum of psalters from the nearby meetinghouse echoed over me as I ate my noon meal on Sunday. The crunch of the juicy apple and the simple taste of squash and corn reminded me of my former life: the bounty of warm and delicious meals I once enjoyed at home. How I wished for ale to wash over my despair and melancholy.

The longer I remained in prison, the more I became like my bleak surroundings. My mind withered, becoming as numb as my hands and feet were at night. I struggled desperately to do what I must to keep up my spirits, with thoughts of my father and our home as my constant companions.

No one could deliver encouragement, and few made any attempt. Lydia was my true friend, but I could not presume much of her. Her physical strength was declining, and extreme melancholy overcame her for days at a time. I gazed upon her as she lay curled up in her blanket on the ground and pictured a vision of my future. We were like the spider web spun above us—so delicate, so sensitive, and so easily damaged.

An invisible force suddenly compelled me to move closer to Lydia. I pulled her shoulders gently until she was sitting upright and rested my face against hers. "Lydia, we must not be overcome with despair. I must resolve to face my scourging with dignity. I want to be like you. You would not whimper. You would call upon all your strength to endure your punishment. My reward will be when the final lash bites through my skin, and I then silently pray, 'God give me the strength and courage to endure what my miserable life has for me now.'"

Lydia's eyes brightened while my tears mixed with hers. She returned to her place on the cold floor with a few strands of straw for solace, and both of us were lulled to sleep by the steady beat of the soft pings of rain.

The days passed into evenings until one morning I was awakened by the sound of hurried steps outside my prison window. Father often walked in the same manner, brisk and loud.

Looking up from my sleep, I saw him. New wrinkles deeply pressed in his forehead exposed his anguish and sleepless nights. He carried new clothes for me with lavender tucked in the folds. My heart leaped with the hope these clothes would take me out of these dank prison walls back to my home.

"Mehitabel, how have you been faring since we last were ..." Father hesitated, "... since we last saw one another." His compassionate nature prompted him to make no mention of my humiliation in the courts of Ipswich.

My weak body strained to stand, and I found it odd that a youth could become so feeble from the adversity of imprisonment. Father should not carry so heavy a burden for my well-being, so I attempted to mask my discomfort and tribulations.

"I have been holding up well, Father. I knew the foods sent each day were from you. Your love and care were in each basket, but there was no sign of you. Have you been unwell these past weeks?"

He held me with a father's tender embrace, so gentle, like one comforting a babe who tumbled on a stone walk.

"Father ..." I sighed, too overwhelmed and weary to utter another word.

"Dear one, I have not been allowed to visit until now. Just this day Major Denison informed me I might come ... to prepare you for tomorrow, Sunday morn."

I glanced up with a slight jolt but was determined to prove I was not the foolish, simple girl spoken of in court. I aspired to be envisaged as a brave and courageous young woman.

"Mehitabel, you will be brought to the post near the hill. Sadly, I tell you, you will receive the whip, but Major Denison assures me you are not deserving of a severe lashing. This is the best news I have for you. You will then spend time in the stocks to bring fairness to your sentence. Still, I wish I could suffer the lash rather than be forced to watch your tender body endure such pain. Oh, how I pray it could be me instead of you, Mehitabel."

Father rocked me again, and I experienced the depth of his love as never before. *Surely, my father will suffer more than I tomorrow.*

I slept through the night and woke only when old Agnes moaned and hacked, but even those sounds strangely soothed me back to rest.

The next morning proved to be dreary as the jailer stood in front of me. He was always a foul fellow, smelling of sour ale. Without a word, he signaled me to follow him and went before me as I trudged up the stairs. I glanced back at the worn blanket, hoping never to lay eyes upon these walls again. Lydia raised her hand to offer some encouragement, but she knew my heart well enough. No words were necessary. I waved farewell, looked upward, and said a prayer for the courage to meet my ordeal with grace.

Familiar faces and strangers from the surrounding villages gathered around the post. I, like most others, had found whipping a perverse spectacle. Although the display was meant to be a warning, it instead made sport of the prisoner's humiliation.

My hands were tightly bound before I was led to the post, where my bindings were then fastened. I scanned the crowd for Father but did not notice him. My witnesses were more in number than Ipswich alone could possibly claim.

Before my lashing, all were to hear a brief sermon of admonition by a pastor from Beverly. His words were only a murmur to my ears, but I stared intently in his direction so as not to impute any disrespect for God's Word or His servant.

That I could act with dignity at this moment was beyond comprehension. I submitted to the crack of each lash, twenty in all. My relative calmness astonished me and all who watched my humiliation. The crowds likely assembled to see a foolish girl scream and curse back at them, but I fixed my gaze firm upon a dark splinter on the post, and there it remained. My body trembled with each lash, but only I could hear my breaths and gentle sighs as I inhaled air to suffer through.

Mercy surely was lavished upon me as only small trickles of blood seeped through my clothing. The jailer untied my hands from the post and likely expected me to faint away, but I stood fast and upright. He then led me to my next humiliation: the pillory.

Another unexpected event lay ahead: the jailer raised the top of the pillory and placed my head and arms through the holes before he lowered the bar. There I stood with my eyes fixed on the bare ground. The crowd lingered just a few minutes as I did not provide the expected show for which they came. A few idle children lingered, but their mothers fetched them after a short time, and then no one remained. My arms and shoulders seared from the pain as my time lingered.

The jailer called for my father. He and Reverend and Mistress Hubbard came forward. They had been standing far behind me. How wise they were to recognize their presence would only intensify my humiliation and sorrow. Father put a cloth on my seething wounds, being careful not to inflame the gashes, and led me to the cart to take me home.

God had come before me. God had prepared my way. God had been with me.

# Chapter Fifteen

The sky darkened as a flock of broad-winged hawks began their southward flight. Our cart rattled past the ripening pumpkins and turnips in the fields, and the click of the wagon's tongue mingled with the horses' steady clip-clop down the winding trail. Every jostle along the road seemed to further open my wounds, firing tremors up my back.

The fragrance of ripened fruit hanging from the apple trees attempted to blow away the painful memories of the past months. They promised a warm home, food on the table, and hope for my future. I gazed at the blue skies and saw a raven carried aloft by the feathering winds, landing deftly on the fence post. The distant howling of wolves from the forest brought me back to reality.

I sought to abandon the darkness with the comforting presence of Margaret Hubbard at my side. We uttered not a word for most of the trip but spoke through the loving tap of her hand upon mine as we rode. The shimmer of the setting sun radiated on our house as Mother's neatly tended garden came into view.

"How are you enduring the pain?" Mistress Hubbard asked. "I have been praying for you these past weeks and begged for God's mercy on you, child. Your path has seen much trouble, but now you can see proof you are greatly loved by our God and have been made rich in His grace."

I felt neither loved nor rich in grace, but her words still comforted me. "I feared much worse, Mother ... I mean, Mistress Hubbard." Overwrought with emotion, tears filled my eyes over my innocent blunder. "You have been so kind and dear to me, like a mother who cares for me."

Mistress Hubbard stroked my hand affectionately, understanding my slip of the tongue.

Sarah and Hannah peered through the kitchen window to witness my return home. Father carried me in his arms to my room and laid my scarred and bloody body upon the bed sack. Mistress Hubbard proceeded to the kitchen to offer instructions and find the necessary items to care for my wounds.

Father disappeared from my side when Mistress Hubbard arrived with Sarah to assist her. With great care, they removed my blood-soaked bodice and bathed my wounds with warm water and applied ointment so they would not reopen. Despite their great care, a few stripes must have ruptured as I began to shake uncontrollably.

Mistress Hubbard entreated me to drink a warm brew, and my tremors ceased. Then she dabbed my wounds with her medicines and oils. "Dear one, be certain to stay on your side. Ask the servants for assistance if you need anything."

After nursing my wounds, Mistress Hubbard and Sarah refreshed my body and spirit by singing Psalms and then prepared to leave so I might rest.

"Mehitabel, dear one," Mistress Hubbard whispered. "I have no words of my own that can ever begin to restore your body and soul. I ask that you call upon the Lord and meditate on His holy words. *Finally, brethren, whatsoever things are true, whatsoever things are honest, whatsoever things are just, whatsoever things are pure, whatsoever things are lovely, whatsoever things are of good report; if there be any virtue, and if there be any praise, think on these things*, Mehitabel."

She stroked my forehead with her soft hand and chanted those words over and over, and with the last whisper, my eyes closed. The searing pain faded into a faraway memory, and I drifted off to sleep.

When my eyes opened again, I knew not how long I slumbered, but the slight flicker of a candle illumined Father's presence. He was next to my bed on a little bench that was much too small for his size. With the sun fully set, the darkness all about told me it was nighttime.

"Father, how have I been able to sleep through such pain? I must have been asleep many hours, but you are here beside me." I reached out for his hand. "How can I thank you? I have brought nothing but shame to you all my life."

Father seemed fearful of touching me at first but then put his hands on mine, seeing they were free from wounds and blood stains. "Mehitabel, a father's love and concern do not end when his child sins or is in need. My heart shared each lash as it was laid upon your body, I assure you. I still suffer your pain."

No more words were necessary as I lay in bed and basked in the certainty of his steadfast love and devotion. The light from the candle flickered in his eyes, and his lips curled into the same smile I recalled from the time I was just a wee girl who made him proud as I recited my verses.

"Dear one, caring for your wounds is just as important as your need for my affections, so I must call Sarah," Father said. She arrived with new linens and balm for my wounds and Hannah brought me a large cup of tea.

"The unique scent of the brew is the reason for my peaceful and sound sleep, is it not, Sarah?" I turned onto my side, the one that suffered fewer lashes, closed my eyes again, and remembered no more.

The next morning, Hannah sprang to her feet from a chair in the corner the moment I stirred. All the linens and healing waters necessary for my morning treatments were on my bed table.

"Mehitabel, I shall return, but let me alert Sarah to fetch your morning meal."

The two servants, just slightly older than me, scurried around my room to open the window and tend to my needs.

"Hannah, Sarah, I thank you for your mercies and tender care. I never understood how difficult the life of a servant was until I became one. I beg your forgiveness if I was ever unkind or inconsiderate."

Hannah and Sarah now seemed more like friends than just servants. Their silent smiles revealed they might consider me as a different, perhaps kinder person, as I now understood their tribulations.

Sarah dabbed each wound, pleased that none reopened. "I have seen much worse, Mehitabel. You were fortunate that Goodman Kinny didn't put his full force into your back as he usually does. You are a blessed girl, indeed."

I offered a slight smile and then asked, "Has my mother been to my room? I may not have been awake when she came to see me."

"Your mother is still about the house, Mehitabel, but gave us instructions on how to prepare your balms and medicines. We did not ask why she did not bring them herself." Sarah bowed her head and looked away.

"And John Beare? Is he still in the house? Is all as it was before?" I queried.

Sarah and Hannah glanced at one another as though uncertain of how to respond. "Things have not quite been the same, but John Beare is still living in this house," Sarah replied.

Hannah, the bolder of the two, interjected, "I overheard John speak of the part of your father's lands promised to him. He may go to the farm in Wenham and begin to seek his own fortune next spring."

I no longer felt hatred toward John Beare, but neither did I bear any affection as a sister or cousin might; I still harbored feelings of resentment when I thought of him. Father's words and actions reassured me that no one, let alone John Beare, would ever take my place in his heart, though it was apparent Father handsomely rewarded John Beare's loyalty.

"One more question. Do you know anything about a woman named Alice we have often seen in the back benches at services? I am not sure where she lives, but you must know who this Alice is."

Sarah and Hannah's expressions grew uneasy, and their eyes met. Sarah's face paled, and her head shook in a small tremor to caution Hannah. "No. I mean, I know of whom you speak, but she is just a woman who must live far away. I think she has a husband. Yes, a husband who is not well. We do not see him, but we see her. But, no, we can tell you nothing ..." With Hannah's garbled words hanging mysteriously in the air, the serving girls left without taking the empty bowls or soiled linens. As they closed the door behind them, I heard the muffled sounds of their panicked voices. I now regretted questioning the servants, but a mystery surrounded this woman I once considered fearful. I grew more curious, as nothing about Alice made much sense to me anymore.

# Chapter Sixteen

Only a few yellow-speckled leaves still clung to their branches. The ever gentle breeze that blew them to the ground announced that cold and misery would soon blanket all of New England. Another proclamation was also clearly made: I would work alongside Sarah and Hannah with their chores. Father insisted.

"Child, you must learn the many duties and responsibilities of a housewife." Father would never say more than that, but it would be only a few years until he and Mother might consider me suitable to marry. I must do much penitence before Father would select a proper husband for me.

I was, however, not alone in my need to seek forgiveness in Ipswich. Each day presented new accusations of fellow sinners in our midst. Robert Crose Jr. almost incited another Indian war when he dug up the grave of Masconomet, the great chief of Agawam. He hoisted the skull on a pole and paraded about the streets with it. For that, he was jailed and whipped. Scurrilous reports of pirates walking freely about town bragging of their ill-gotten goods were common. Even worse were reports that some of the merchants near the ports traded with these scoundrels.

Perhaps my tribulations and sins would be just a meager memory as the ranks of sinners grew.

Mother was constantly beset by melancholy and remained in her bed much during the day, or sat in her chair and stared out the window. She permitted no one save the servants to enter our home to visit and went to no other home, even when the neighbor women invited her. Mother never uttered my name and spoke to me only through the servants. Clearly, my crime hurled her spirits into the ocean's abyss.

Two pumpkins were clenched under each arm as I entered through the main door. I attempted to close the door while precariously balancing my load, but one crashed to the floor with the seeds and pulp flying all over. *Right in front of Mother!*

"I'm sorry, Mother. They were heavier than I expected. I suppose my one arm just gave out."

Mother threw her head back against the seat in disgust, "Just clean it up! Another one of your blunders."

I set the other pumpkin on the table and retrieved a rag and bucket to clean up the mess.

A voice in the back of my mind cautioned restraint, but my foolish nature was still able to rear its ugly head. "Why do you treat me like this? Why would someone who insists I call her Mother spread scurrilous tales about me to all the women of the village? You never once came to visit me in prison, and the old hags there repeated all of your stories about me over and over. You are a gossip, and the Bible says …"

"Do not quote Scripture to me, Mehitabel! Scripture says a father's sin is carried down to his children, and his children's children, so remember that! You are the spawn of your father and his whore; you are not my child."

I didn't cry, as I had heard those words so many times before. I wanted to argue, to tell her of the pain she had caused me. I wished any other woman in Ipswich could be my mother instead of her, but quarreling with Mother would be more than foolish. I wiped the floor until not one sign of flesh or seeds remained, and then I went outside to find Sarah and Hannah, my only link to the outside world.

John Beare's presence in the house created a constant cloud of hostility. When John entered the house, he would open the door and peer around with darting glances to see if I was about. He then scurried to another room or turned heel and left the house if I was nearby. I tried to consider what words would make amends, but both Mother's and John Beare's eyes spoke hatred about the shame I brought to the Braybrooke family.

Our walks from the cart to the church meetinghouse on Sundays were different than before. When I was younger, Mother forced me to sit next to her at each Sunday meeting, displaying me as the curse she must bear and made sure to discipline me if I so much as shifted my body to one side. I had not joined our congregation since my time with the Chipmans, and Mother kept herself at a distance. Father positioned me to his right on my first Sunday back and Mother to his left. As we entered, he said, "Mehitabel, your wounds are fully recovered, and you can now endure the many hours of sitting on the bench. Listen carefully to the reverend's messages, as his words of admonition are for those who need much repentance."

We all parted ways once inside—Father with the men and Mother with the women. Sarah and Hannah welcomed me to the servants' benches.

After the service, Mistress Hubbard approached me to ask how I fared and to impart a Scripture passage. Her selections were always as if she could read my mind and soul.

Early December was an ideal time for venison stew, plump with turnips and barley and seasoned with rosemary. The task would be completely mine to demonstrate my new talent with herbs and root vegetables. The creak of the front door hinge announced Father was home.

"Mehitabel, I have been looking for you. Come for a stroll; the day beckons us," he said.

"I only have to add the salt, and I shall join you outside in just a moment," I replied.

It was indeed a delightful December day. The bright sun warmed our cloaks while the geese flew overhead as we sauntered past the gardens.

I expected we would take the path to inspect the animals grazing in the distant fields, but Father and I walked only until our farm faded out of view. We spoke of many things of no real consequence, but then he cleared his throat. "Mehitabel, Sarah tells me that you have been working as one of the servants, with proper diligence and spirit these past weeks. It makes me proud to hear such excellent reports of your recovery and restoration, and it lifts my spirits to see you reading Scriptures during these dark, lonely nights. Your countenance as of late beams brightly, showing you are gaining wisdom. Have you now left your childhood follies behind?"

"Father, yes, my future tells me I must grow as a godly young woman and leave my childish ways in the past. I indeed have been seeking that."

With a gentle push on my shoulder, Father signaled me to sit on a newly hewn stump of an old oak. He spoke into the bright skies with his hands clenched behind his back. "Mehitabel, you must know you cannot expect to live in the house with your mother and me much longer. The darkness of your mother's condition gives me much fear. I have sacrificed for her health, but she worsens in body and spirit. As her husband, I have hurt her in many ways." He hesitated and looked in my direction. "It is best we secure a husband for you, Mehitabel. Soon."

I sprang from the stump and turned away, covering my mouth. Father's proposal left me in disbelief.

"Father, I have been seeking to gain the skills of a good wife, a godly wife for someone who might have no knowledge of my sins. He could be a man not yet here in Ipswich but still in England or, perhaps, a far-off village. Someone who would only see the better person I am trying to become. I am not yet seventeen; I'm not ready, Father!"

"Mehitabel, all you say are dreams. God has smitten us, and we must turn our faces to Him and be obedient to what He demands."

"A young woman of my age only marries if she is with child." The desperation in my voice intensified. "Father, I will work harder and plow in the fields this spring and summer if only you allow me to stay with you. Mother will surely see I have repented, and my face has turned completely toward God's will."

"Mehitabel, your words cannot change my resolve. Your sins have affected not just you but many others. My heart must close to your wishes. We will visit Reverend and Mistress Hubbard tomorrow. They have proposed a suitable husband for you. I cannot tell you more, but I promise to provide details as soon as I arrange your dowry."

# CHAPTER SEVENTEEN

The prospect of such an early marriage was something I never considered. Young women all over New England did not typically marry until twenty-one, and even that age was close to improper. A far worse destiny than marriage at age sixteen would be to become an indentured servant in a faraway village. My options were few.

My mind inventoried the worst and lowliest of men who might consider me. Throughout the colony were vile, filthy men who drank heavily and returned from the taverns, taking out their miserable existence upon their poor wives. I could not foresee any prospects beyond the wretched men in the village who menaced young women with their lusty eyes.

True to his word the next morning, Father signaled it was time for our visit with Reverend Hubbard, and he then went to ready the horses. Mother stood on the landing with her hands on her hips and launched into a tirade even before I descended the stairs. "Mehitabel, listen—do not talk back. Make no comments to the Hubbards other than to beg forgiveness, agree, and then offer thanksgiving for our minister's considerable efforts. You have made everyone's life bitter with so many troubles and woes for our family. Remember, you will do as you are told!"

With those harsh words of chastisement, Mother turned and went to the kitchen where she fussed with Hannah and Sarah while they packed the loaves of bread and cheese for the Hubbards. Sarah carried the basket to Father, and we put on our cloaks to set out for our journey to the village.

The fragrant air steamed above the linen-covered basket as we traveled on the path to meet with the Hubbards. Inside were freshly made loaves filled with the best spices and choicest fruits available this time of year. In years past, I had always experienced a pleasant ambiance when I traveled to the Hubbards' home, which rested upon the knoll. This trip teemed with doom and trepidation.

We trekked a great distance before speaking any words. Father stopped to observe a huge flock of blackbirds circling an unusual area east of Jeffrey's Neck and wondered what attracted those annoying rascals. We spoke of the hope of an early spring to tease the flow of sap from our sugar maples. Our trivial observations made it evident I was not to inquire about the details to be discussed with the Hubbards. Mother shook her head in frustration, visibly annoyed with our chatter.

The smell of stately pines planted in straight and proper rows graced the impressive path to the Hubbards' home. Bright green holly bushes bursting with berries contrasted against the gray stonework on the house's exterior. Father grabbed the polished brass knocker on the grand entrance door of the house, but hesitated and then turned to offer last-minute advice before he signaled the Hubbards' servants. "Mehitabel, I have no apprehension about this matter. I ask you to only listen and have a pleasant countenance. We will talk about the young man on our way home."

The Hubbards greeted us with their usual refined manners and appeared genuinely glad to see me. Perhaps, I thought, there might be just a twinge of pleasant news in store for me. I entered their home for the first time as a young woman, rather than a child or discarded servant.

Little in their home had changed since my childhood visits. The bright sunlight beamed through the windows to make the dusty air dance. The oak cupboards and imported chests displayed the elegant pewter and china pieces Mistress Hubbard inherited from her father. I now could appreciate the tedious work required from the servants to maintain the well-ordered house of Ipswich's most esteemed family.

"Mehitabel, you have pleased both your parents and God with your desire to seek forgiveness with a contrite heart. You look well." Reverend Hubbard stopped short of inquiring about my physical well-being.

"I thank you, Reverend Hubbard, and your wife also. I know you have been praying for my soul and my healing." I said no more as I was instructed only to listen.

Mother chose a seat in a secluded corner of the room. Her sullen disposition was no stranger to any of us, and her rigid pose encouraged no one to invite her into the conversation.

Father sat across from me. "Reverend Hubbard, I have informed Mehitabel you wish to discuss a proposition to secure a suitable husband for her. Her mother and I are grateful you have been both helpful and discreet in this matter."

Reverend Hubbard leaned back in his chair with his arms folded. "Richard, Joan, I have called upon two young men in town. They are both of a proper age to seek a wife, but I fear they have shown little inclination on their own. I spoke to them as their minister. Neither has a father to guide them, to encourage them in such matters. One of the men seemed more than agreeable to my proposition. I feared our discussion would end with the mention of the bride's name, but he gave me encouragement to proceed."

My heart tingled with a twinge of hope that the Hubbards had found a suitable husband for me. Perhaps he was not a vulgar old man whom I would find repulsive. I considered the few kind and humble bachelors who worked as hired hands or men just released from their indenture. Perhaps he would be a young man like Jacob Perkins.

"The young man of whom I am speaking is one my wife has known for … well, Margaret, has it been almost his whole life?"

"Yes, William. But I can see by the look on Mehitabel's face she is desperate to learn his name. Husband, let us tell her a bit about him first." Mrs. Hubbard's smile grew wide as if to deliver a gift she hoped would be well received.

"Margaret, I will ask you to tell his story since you know him so well. Mehitabel will then determine if she considers the young man a suitable choice for her husband." Reverend Hubbard sat back in his chair to allow Margaret to speak.

"First, Mehitabel, I am certain you have seen him for many years, and he is perhaps ten years your senior. It is true Reverend Hubbard and I needed to encourage him to consider his duty and responsibilities as a godly man to secure a wife. He has been preoccupied with tending his lands and spends much time with his brother—"

"Of which we do not approve," William Hubbard interrupted. "Young men need to pursue the path of righteousness and not foolish ways. This arrangement is God's choice for him, I am certain." Reverend Hubbard's face revealed that this man might have a flaw, but many a young man these days demonstrated no hurry to enter into marriage. Reverend Hubbard's sermons taught us marriage was a solemn relationship bringing either great joy or unending sorrow and grief.

"Dear husband," Margaret smiled, showing no criticism of her husband's warning. She proceeded to make the grand announcement so as not to incur another discouraging word from Reverend Hubbard. "Mehitabel, John Downing has agreed he would consider calling on you and your household to become better acquainted, but he gave us no fast assurance. He seemed amenable to our proposal."

*"John Downing … John Downing!"* My mind repeated the words over and over. Complete joy rushed over me with a visible shiver. My broad smile let all know of not only my relief but my utter delight.

Mistress Hubbard crooked her head and smiled, sharing my obvious happiness. Mother sat silently, rubbing her lower lip between her thumb and forefinger, then stood and left the room without a word. Her abrupt departure needed no explanation. It was against Mother's nature to be happy for me.

Reverend Hubbard's somber words brought us all back to the reality of what we must now consider. "Mehitabel, you must be aware that John Downing comes from one of the most esteemed families who ever lived in Ipswich. It has been perhaps … has it been fifteen or more years since his parents left the final time? When the Downings departed, there was no intention of returning. Lucy,

Emanuel's wife, found living in the colonies tedious and much too dangerous. Emanuel has gone to his eternal reward, buried in Scotland for about the past ten years. I understand Lucy's current efforts have centered on her son in London. Sir George Downing serves in the highest circles in court."

Margaret interrupted her husband in her typical genteel way. Apparently, she did not want to give Father too high an opinion concerning John Downing's status in Ipswich. "John tells us he has not received any direct correspondence from his mother in several years. He lived with my family for several years after Emanuel entrusted his son's care to my dear father, Nathaniel Rogers. Mehitabel, I have known John since he was a lad. He grew up thinking of me as his older sister, which I was in many ways."

Father sat as still as a deer stares before returning to the woods. His silence revealed his misgivings of this arrangement, and I understood his concern. I gave John Downing far too much attention when we were growing up. I was then a silly little child, and John more than ten years older than I. Father may fear that my folly might stir again.

I could only imagine a man like John would be a perfect and most agreeable husband. It was as if the king had granted me the hand of his most adored son. My lone fear was that John might not consider me a suitable wife.

Mistress Hubbard hurried me to the hallway entrance to fill my ears with Scriptures about marriage and a wife's duties. I strained to hear what Father and Reverend Hubbard were discussing. The words of the Reverend were clear as he imparted his final instructions. "Richard, you understand about the lands. The details of the contract will now be between you and John Downing."

Father helped me fix my cape properly as we readied to depart. Then the Reverend added, "Mehitabel, the Lord will go ahead of you. Keep your good senses. I am much afraid that this marriage contract may be the only suitable one I can arrange for you." Reverend Hubbard's firm look indicated I best heed the seriousness of his words.

"Reverend, Mistress Hubbard, I make a vow to you that I have mended my ways and only seek God's will, grace, and provision with all my heart and soul. I vow not to disappoint you."

"Mehitabel," cautioned Reverend Hubbard, "God tells us not to make a vow. Let your yes be yes, and your no be no."

With those cautionary words of Scripture, which I had never really understood, Father, Mother, and I walked to our carriage. I sauntered along behind my parents as they discussed the details of the Hubbards' proposal. I heard none of it as their chatter dissipated into the clouds. My heart and mind flew to the heavens as a bird ascends into the air on a new spring day.

# CHAPTER EIGHTEEN

How I wanted to flutter to my room like a tiny purple finch to entertain pleasant thoughts about John Downing as my future husband. Instead, I embraced Reverend Hubbard's caution to not revert to the silly girl I once had been. My assistance with the evening meal's preparation seemed a more prudent first step.

Sarah and Hannah rushed to greet me, and the news of a courtship spilled from my lips. Hannah's smile showed genuine happiness for me. "Now you will never be a thornback shriveled up in your Father's house surrounded only by servants."

Sarah added, "Aye, my mother used to caution us girls, saying, 'Women dying maids lead apes in Hell.' Oh, that image keeps me on the straight path for a suitable marriage contract!"

At dinner, Mother joined Father and me for the first time since my return. Perhaps she might approve of or even bless my marriage. I must not be involved in frivolous chatter, but it was challenging to contain my happiness.

Father announced John Downing would visit in two days. He placed a box in front of me. "This is a gift John sent for you. John also dispatched Mother a box of exotic fruits, which seem quite mysterious. I am told they are called shattucks, but we are not sure if they are food to be eaten or if they are ornamental." Father chuckled at this delightful dilemma. "John secured them from a trader in Barbados."

The servants huddled by the kitchen door to have a peek at my treasure, but Mother's stony glare made them all retreat. In the box was a lovely turquoise fan with embroidered designs. I opened the blades to display its full beauty.

Father said, "I believe the fan was made to look like a peacock, and the color is the same as your eyes. This fan is a most wonderful gift, Mehitabel. Your meeting with John Downing should go well."

"Don't be a stupid girl when he arrives," Mother interrupted in a scolding tone. "Have the fan in your hands the entire time he is here, to show your gratitude." I knew to smile and agree with Mother, but her advice on how to display my appreciation was unnecessary. Still, Mother's presence at dinner was an encouraging sign.

"Mother, I would be grateful if you could give me instructions on manners and the skills of a good wife if John is agreeable to begin courting." I gave her a soft smile and attempted to show humility.

"Just say little and stay out of trouble till the magistrate fully covenants you. That is all I have to say."

My heart sank, although I should have anticipated her response. My only hope was to learn from Mistress Hubbard.

As the two days passed by, my thoughts often wandered to John Downing. How should I present myself, what should I wear, and what should I say? I feared he might ask about my time in prison or my months as a serving girl. I rehearsed Scripture for my responses to show I was a transformed woman who had fully repented of my sins. He must never know of the horrors I suffered.

So many details were necessary to create the proper impression for John's visit. Sarah, Hannah, and I prepared an excellent stew of young duck and root vegetables accompanied by fruits, bread, and cheeses. John Downing must perceive me as a sweet and agreeable young woman whom he might grow to love. I would imitate the woman I most admired, Margaret Hubbard, and emulate her calmness, her hand movements, and especially the sweetness of her voice.

My heart quickened upon hearing the knock on the door. There stood the dashing John Downing, and Father greeted him with gracious enthusiasm. John removed his elegant, wide-brimmed hat to reveal his brown hair, fashionably long and tousled. He surveyed our hall, furnished in a grand style of tapestries, pewter, and finely carved chests and chairs. Hopefully, this finery would assure John I came from a household worthy of marriage to a son of Emanuel Downing.

Father led John to a chair near the hearth as our servants readied the midday meal, and said, "Mehitabel made a great effort cooking this sumptuous meal."

I felt the warm blush on my cheeks. Hopefully, John might see me as humble. He maintained a pleasant but serious manner with Father as they spoke of the political affairs in Boston and the latest news of Indian uprisings in York. They stopped when the details became increasingly violent, as genteel women should not hear of such reports.

Father rose to escort Mother to the table, and John flashed a quick smile and gestured for me to enter before him. His elegant manners revealed that his father Emanuel and Nathaniel Rogers had, indeed, raised him to be a gentleman.

Sarah presented the bread and stew, placing our finest linens at each person's side. The thick and savory stew was much improved since I last checked. Hannah had added her special touches and herbs, taking care to stir the kettle so not one tender morsel scorched. I flashed an affirming nod when she came out to refresh our drink.

The discourse at the meal was pleasant, although we discussed little of consequence. Everyone was aware of the topics to avoid. John glanced in my direction with a smile. The advice for me to be silent was well-considered.

"Goodman and Goodwife Braybrooke, I thank you for your gracious hospitality, and Mehitabel, the ducks flying above your farm must be enchanted. This was the finest stew I have ever tasted," said John.

Father's timing was exquisite. "John, you are welcome to join us this Sunday for services or whenever you feel the time may be right," Father said with only slight trepidation. "Please also join us for our meal on the Holy Sabbath," I worried Father's request, while well intended, might be premature. Such an invitation would signal the congregation that our courtship had commenced.

John, however, responded enthusiastically with a firm handshake, "Sir, I find your request to be most welcome and gratifying."

My heart sweetly stirred upon hearing John's reply, and my mind no longer found room for any trivial worries.

# CHAPTER NINETEEN

Had the curse I bore from birth lifted? I carefully considered my next steps, determined to assure my marriage to John would take place. My only skills as a homemaker were what Mother taught me about herbs and plants and what I garnered from our servants. I was resolute to watch and listen more carefully when Mother gave directions to Sarah and Hannah, and I hoped Mistress Hubbard might take me under her wing. John Downing had inherited sufficient lands in Salem to earn the distinctive title of planter, and I knew I must show I was worthy to be called his wife.

In early June, I asked John if he had written to Lucy Downing about our future marriage. His countenance immediately changed to one of sadness. "Mother's letters to me are through her lawyers in Boston. She gives them instructions on how to manage her holdings, and I send a report through them. That is all I write, except a pleasant greeting and a loving ending saying she is missed."

John sighed deeply. "Mother's attentions are only on her eldest son, Sir George Downing. News of my brother's high office and influence is frequently mentioned. When she left the colonies, Mother put an ocean between herself and her children left behind. Mother left a pittance of love behind when she returned to England. We have learned this situation is no great burden."

"It appears you have made an uneasy peace with your mother," I said.

"Cromwell's victory at the time of my parents' departure assured all who called themselves Puritans that England was safe. Father and George's political ambitions were secured, and my parents returned to Mother England after living in this colony for twenty years. Their former house and land holdings in Ipswich continue to remind the townspeople of my parents' substantial influence."

I would never live up to Lucy Downing's level of refinement and intelligence. Known for her legendary wit as a lively hostess, Lucy was well-versed in all the skills one might observe in the royal circles in London. John told me his mother wrote several long letters each afternoon and enjoyed dining with New England's most learned people.

"In response to your question about our future as man and wife, I expect her attorneys in Boston will soon give notice of our courtship to my mother."

I simply nodded in agreement and allowed John to steer the course of our destiny.

"Mehitabel, my wish is that our courtship not last past this summer. I know you are quite young for marriage. I am not ignorant of such but fear we should not prolong our courtship. My inheritance may be at risk if we wait much longer. My stepbrother James has experienced Mother's wrath, with her attorney's reports of his drinking. She holds his estate in the balance, threatening to withdraw his rights. In fact, James has few rights, considering his position as her stepson."

My heart and mind were aflutter as our courtship proceeded at a rapid pace, but I hadn't considered John's delicate position. To the people of Ipswich, he seemed to be a prosperous heir, but Lucy Downing could change John's inheritance and withdraw his landholdings with the stroke of a pen. I resolved to show myself as a young lady worthy of a marriage contract with a son from an influential family. Every villager must perceive me as a laudable and praiseworthy daughter-in-law if Lucy or her attorneys should inquire.

In July, John was intent on moving forward with a contraction of marriage and wanted to talk about a date for our betrothal ceremony. Mother denied us the right to bundle, which was a great disappointment to both John and me. We simply wished to lie quietly with one another in a chaste manner through the night as did most other betrothed in New England. To become better acquainted with John and to speak freely with him was my only desire. Certainly, God blessed Ruth and Boaz when they spent the night together on a threshing room floor. Like so many of my other requests, Mother would not hear of it.

My parents finally permitted us to talk in private while they watched from a distance. Mother was still concerned I might talk foolishly and give John doubts about marriage to me. John and I walked to the edge of the barn and glanced around to assure ourselves we were not within hearing distance of the servants.

John asked to hold my right hand. "Mehitabel, we have never spoken of our past, but I have known you would be my wife since you were a young blonde-haired girl at church meetings stealing glances at me. You know you stared at me, did you not?" John's smile broadened as his eyes softened. "I remember my thoughts from those years. I knew you would grow into a beautiful young woman with whom I would wish to share my life."

A tingling sensation swept over my body. "John, I thought of you as being so much more commendable than I, like how a girl might imagine the king's son. But you must also know of my past sins and my crime. I was a foolish girl, filled with envy and bitterness, but my pain has taught me much. I will prove myself a worthy wife who will make even your mother look away from my past … if she hears of it."

John smiled tenderly and caressed my hand. "Mehitabel, I went away to my house in Salem the summer of your punishment. I did not wish to see you scourged, and your grace and calmness of spirit served to quiet the tongues of those who once wished you great harm and humiliation. Mehitabel, my love, I believe God wishes us to be yoked together, and I am in full agreement with His will."

We strolled toward Father and Mother with our arms linked to signal an announcement could soon be made. "Goodman Braybrooke, Goody Braybrooke, we have good news for you. Mehitabel and I ask that you arrange a betrothal ceremony. It is our wish to be married soon, before harvest."

"The banns of marriage can be posted on the church door the next Sunday?" asked Father. Pulling John to his side, Father shook his hand heartily and overtook the conversation. The two men walked with good cheer as they spoke of our plans. Mother walked silently next to me, and I could feel her spirits lift. Their chatter was of no concern to her, and so the men continued inside our home.

Mother and I stopped at the door, and before we entered, she spoke. "You know what John Downing is asking of Father, do you not? He is much afraid of losing his landholdings if Lucy Downing discovers her son has chosen so poor a wife. John is shrewd and set his eyes upon the pretty daughter of a man who has sizeable lands. You, Mehitabel, will cost your father much of *our* good fortune just to rid our lives of you. Heed my words; you will not get another shilling of our wealth once you are John's burden. I can only say that my great reward in all of this is to have some pittance of peace when I no longer have to suffer from the sores of your curse."

With those bitter words, Mother went into her room where she would not have to cast her eyes upon me.

It grieved me that Father was compelled to give far beyond the usual bride price for my dowry, but it was a great favor for John to accept so wretched a girl for his wife. How fortunate I was to be born into a home of privilege and some wealth. How woeful it must be for Father to see his wealth squandered on the jail fines and an excessive bride price, all because of his sinful daughter.

The next day, Father spoke with Reverend Hubbard, who greeted the news as no surprise. Mistress Hubbard extended a special invitation to help me choose the text of Scripture for Reverend Hubbard's sermon at our betrothal party. I accepted her offer, although I had already selected the verses from Ephesians. All in attendance should understand I wished to be the kind of wife expressed in Scripture:

*Wives, submit yourselves unto your own husbands, as unto the Lord. For the husband is the head of the wife, even as Christ is the head of the church: and He is the saviour of the body. Therefore as the church is subject unto Christ, so let the wives be to their own husbands in everything. Husbands, love your wives, even as Christ also loved the church, and gave himself for it; that He might sanctify and cleanse it with the washing of water by the word, that He might present it to himself a glorious church, not having spot, or wrinkle, or any such thing; but that it should be holy and without blemish.*

*So ought men to love their wives as their own bodies. He that loveth his wife loveth himself. For no man ever yet hated his own flesh; but nourisheth and cherisheth it, even as the Lord the church: For we are members of his body, of his flesh, and of his bones. For this cause shall a man leave his father and mother, and shall be joined unto his wife, and they two shall be one flesh.*

Our banns of marriage were published, and John and I became man and wife on September 2, 1669, with our signing the clerk's book. Our guests joined us at my father's home to celebrate with bridal cakes and a cup of sack posset.

We were now married, just as we both imagined long ago. Surely all our days would be summer.

# Chapter Twenty

Our first year of marriage exceeded all my expectations. Mother's harsh words for John's reasons to have me as his wife still weighed heavy on my heart, but I never doubted his love. I kept secret my concern about my excessive bride price. John assured me I was the prettiest wife in all of Ipswich and bought me silks and laces to prove his dedication. Our home was modest but still fitting of his status of a planter.

John's pleasant and outgoing ways gained him many friends who spoke respectfully of his acute business sense. He had not attended Harvard as had his brother George. The opportunity for George to study with pious and learned men who held strong Puritan beliefs convinced Emanuel and Lucy to move to the Massachusetts Colony. Harvard was considered far superior to the less rigorous education George would have obtained at Oxford. "Raucous frivolity and drinking" were the great distractions for scholars in London. Oxford was certainly not a school pious Puritans chose as the most esteemed opportunity for their sons.

In his early years in Ipswich, John received instruction at the grammar school attended by the sons of the well-educated men in the villages. He was schooled in Greek and Latin, various histories, mathematics, and classical works, but academic endeavors were of scant interest to John as he grew into manhood.

James, John's older stepbrother, was a disappointment to his father. Embarrassed about James' writing skills, Emanuel called it "scribbling nonsense." He believed time at school was lost on James. Emanuel even threatened to have James employed as a servant to Governor John Winthrop, Lucy's brother. James made a great effort to associate himself with the well-trained men in Salem. Unfortunately, he was found lacking and covertly mocked as a failure who imbibed too much in rum and hard liquors.

A frequent visitor to our home, James treated me with cautious respect. He had been a spectator at my whipping with full awareness of my crimes. He and I shared deep shame—his love of alcohol and my sinful past.

In early winter, John received news of the dreaded visit from Lucy Downing's attorney. Neither James nor John held any real responsibility for management of Lucy's holdings in the colonies. Instead, Mr. Samuel Stone administered her affairs. He was a most amiable man, but John understood his agreeable nature might serve to trick him into a misstep.

Mr. Stone expected John and James to be present when he came to visit in late December. James arrived the night before Mr. Stone's visit to stay as a guest in our home. He staggered into our house and fell into a chair.

John shook his head. "Too much drink at the ordinary? James, I will help you to your room, but you must present yourself in good order to Mr. Stone. We'll have none of this tomorrow!"

Mr. Stone arrived promptly the next morning. I was not invited to join the men but could hear every word from the next room. His serious tone gave me to fear the worst.

"Sirs, I bring news from your mother. She continues to enjoy the protection of the king through her son George who has secured friends in esteemed and royal circles. King Charles looks upon George as one whose loyalties have never been in doubt. You may not be aware that George received a full pardon for his misjudgment as a spy for Cromwell. George laid blame on the godly men of Massachusetts for what he calls false ideas he learned while in the colonies."

Mr. Stone could not hide his disdain for George's cutting accusation. George was a political opportunist who would switch loyalties as it suited him. His contempt for the esteemed teachers and respected ministers in the colonies who mentored him was despicable. Mr. Stone shook his head with disdain and with a muffled, angry voice said, "May God forgive him."

He shuffled through some papers to gain composure and cleared his throat. "George will soon be appointed the ambassador to the Netherlands, and his shrewd business dealings in the Indies have given him great prosperity. Your mother is most proud."

Neither James nor John gave any reaction to Mr. Stone's news, as George's good fortune and his mother's pride in her eldest son were no news at all. Her other children's shortcomings were always measured against the towering achievements of George, despite reports of his reputation as a conniver and outright liar. His abandonment of our Puritan principles had placed him in the position of a traitor, and colonists spoke of his name with derision. He turned his back on all Puritans and Cromwell to curry favor with the king, and that strategy served him well.

"Now, to move on to the instructions from your mother. She directed me to place John's lands and current home under a special trust administered solely by her representatives in Salem. John, you are to move onto the dowry lands you have rights to from your marriage contract. I fear your mother's memory of her own home being burned to the ground in Salem those many years ago influenced her feelings about your choice of a wife. She has received many letters about Mehitabel's part in the fire at the Perkins home. I know for certain the Perkinses informed her of your marriage. Lucy views your marriage as a union that has brought disgrace to the Downing family."

Mr. Stone gave a heavy sigh. "John, you had to have known of such a consequence. The letters gave your mother full knowledge of Mehitabel's past depravities, and she was already aware of Richard's sin of fornication from her early years in Ipswich."

Mr. Stone then turned to James. "James, your stepmother has all but given up on your soul. She demands you return to Salem and have no contact with Mehitabel. It greatly distresses her that your propensity to sin might increase from any association with the Braybrookes. I am to make arrangements for you to live with a suitable family in Salem, but she cautions that you are not to come to England. Lucy further instructs that any attempt to not abide by her demands will put you outside any future inheritance."

James pounded his fist on the table and leaned toward Mr. Stone. "Sir, these reports are distortions and false. God forgives all who have made errors, especially the sins of pious people such as the Braybrookes. This news leaves me in ruins and could never have been my father's intent when he left John and me in Ipswich like orphans. It is quite clear Lucy Downing has despised me since the day she became my stepmother."

Mr. Stone's expression was as his name's meaning, and he lowered his head. It was true Emanuel and Lucy were esteemed in the colonies for these many years, she the sister of a governor and Emanuel a diligent lawyer from London. They failed their children left behind in Ipswich by leaving the hard work of parenting to those whose burdens were already great. *May God forgive Lucy Downing for her sins against Emanuel's sons.*

Mr. Stone's parting counsel for John was for him to speak immediately to Father and assert his rights to the land promised in my bridal contract. I shuddered. *Might John want to secure a divorce to curry favor with his mother?* Mr. Stone's departing steps rang terror in my heart as I waited for John to find me.

My curse had not evaporated. It now passed on to my beloved John. Satan was alive and well in Ipswich, in Salem, and in London.

# Chapter Twenty-One

John and I moved into a small house on the westerly side of the Ipswich-Gloucester boundary line after Father arranged for the tenants to leave. The structure was just two rooms, but John promised to add onto it after our crops could be sold. We would build a home with two stories much like the one we were forced to leave.

The following days were difficult as my husband toiled alongside our servants rather than oversee them in the fields. John rarely spoke harsh or complaining words and only lamented that his upbringing did not equip him for such strenuous labor.

James Downing returned to Salem, and we heard nothing of him until we received news of his death. He had been killed, but not by Indians as we had once feared. James "traveled with his rum on the road to perdition" as Reverend Hubbard would say. John's deep sadness over his brother's death wounded him as if a hole was carved into his soul.

"Mehitabel, your eyes are not on your food this morning. You were awake before the sun rose, and your complexion is not well. I have concerns for your well-being, wife." John studied me for an answer to soothe his obvious worries. "Your disposition has been such for many weeks. I believe we should consult the physician."

It was true; my samp was put aside each morning, and I could not bear to eat one spoonful. There was no need for John to worry, as I was flourishing. During our growing years, neither John nor I had witnessed the condition of a woman with child.

John should be told, but I had not consulted with any goodwife who could offer her wisdom. Neither Mother nor I were ever called upon to assist when neighbor women met their time of travail. Mother despised the entire birthing process, bitter and envious of others' fruitfulness.

I was sure of it now. God blessed me with a child in my womb. "John, this discomfort I have will soon pass." I rose from the table to put my arms around his shoulders and kissed his neck. "John, do you not see? I am with child. I am certain of it!"

John's body was lifeless for only a few moments, and then he pulled me gently onto the bench beside him. "So, it is natural to feel so melancholy and wretched at the start of each day?"

"John, I have never observed others suffering what I am going through. I shall speak with Mistress Hubbard. But, are you happy of this news, John?"

The smile on John's face was all I needed to know his answer. "My love, a child is always a blessing …"

"John, there is no greater happiness for me than this. The two of us have become three, and now we are one family, just like God intended."

My voice trailed off at the thought of how a child was surely God's wish for all women. The babe in me was a sign of His blessing. *May God grant us a quiver full of children! My wee one will never bear the belief that he or she was born a curse.*

Mistress Hubbard was the first person I told of our good news. Immediately, her concerns were for my health, assuring me such feelings were natural. We discussed what I would need: the herbs and medicines to have on hand, the birthing linens, and the food choices for the proper health of my unborn child.

Weary of the never-ending winter snow, Father's visit early that bitter March morning lifted my spirits. John asked for Father's opinion on the plans for next year's planting, and they sat discussing the necessary rotations and boundary issues that had arisen with our neighbors. From a distance, I made merry in the kitchen, hardly able to contain my happiness. My steps were like dancing as I brought bread and cheese to the table for our first meal of the day.

"Father, John and I wish to bring you good news, and it isn't about the crops but of breeding." He peered at me with a quizzical expression. After that sly suggestion, I said, "Father, I have a verse I have been saving for you. It is from Proverbs: *Children's children are the crown of old men; and the glory of children are their fathers.* Surely, you—"

Father stood and smiled with his arms out wide, clearly comprehending the meaning.

"But you, dear Father, are not aged," I said as he tenderly embraced me.

"Mehitabel, my dear child, now a mother soon to be. When should we expect the baby to come into the world?" Father asked, with the glow I had hoped to see.

"September. If a boy, we wish to name him Charles, after our great king of England. If a girl, we have considered a few names from the Old Testament but have not as yet agreed. John and I are pleased to honor you with a grandchild. You have been a godly father to us both."

My joy was overwhelming, but I needed to develop deeper friendships with the neighbor women. I trusted they would look kindly on my news, which would soon be no secret. My wish was always to be considered a responsible and loving wife and not just a newly married girl. I was not yet eighteen and considered by most too young to marry and give birth, but all who counted the months would know I brought no scandal to my family.

There were a few shrews in the village who continued only to remember my sins, but I slowly gained favor with others through acts of mercy and kindness. Father provided me with the means to bestow proper gifts upon the women who might give aid at my time of travail. Mistress Hubbard did all she could to speak well of me and remind others that God hides our sins once we have fully repented. I was determined to be as white as snow.

# CHAPTER TWENTY-TWO

Charles Downing was born in September of 1670. As busy as life was during these times, the blessing of motherhood gave my life new purpose. I was inwardly ashamed that my desire was to be nothing like my stepmother. In fact, I used her as an example of how not to mother. I grew bitter remembering how I was denied a mother's tender love and arms. Joan's apathy toward Charles stung like a wasp in my heart but seemed strangely natural, as I expected little from her.

Father made a great effort to visit each day and bask in the glory of his grandson. He called him "The King" when no servants were nearby to overhear his playful name for Charles. Father held my son with such affection, and I imagined how he must have first embraced me when he brought me home. Father had not been like other Puritan fathers—stiff and aloof. He never demanded my will should be broken to raise me as a godly child. His tender embrace was all I ever knew.

So many questions dwelt in my mind as I cared for Charles. What harsh words had Joan whispered into my infant ears, of the anger and bitterness she felt toward my birth mother and me? Did I suckle for days or weeks at my own mother's breast before I came to live with Father and Joan? Was a wet nurse employed to care for my needs as a babe? I never realized how utterly helpless infants were, nor their many demands. Yet a loving mother's embrace could soothe most needs. I held my sweet babe and often cried silent tears, imagining how I was likely neglected as an infant. Was it my plight to lie alone for hours at a time as the cloud of Joan's hostility rained down on me?

I never pondered the possibility of these sad, buried events during my youthful years. Now I often contemplated my real mother. To speak of her or to ask questions about her identity was a path always denied me. I desired to know her name, but it would bring shame upon my father to mention his sins. I no longer much feared the wrath of Mother. Nothing I had ever done led me to her approbation, and her ever-ready anger bothered me little. I kept the hope that one day I would know about my real mother buried in my heart.

Joan rarely came with Father to visit. The villagers knew her temperament and did not inquire of her, nor did they expect to see Joan holding Charles in her arms. She gave a faint smile and told others of her worries that her back ailments might cause her to drop our baby. "To see Charles growing strong and well is a blessing for us all. We pray God's protection over him," was all Joan would say.

My heart had some empathy for Joan as I pondered how she must have suffered all the years after Father's betrayal of his marriage covenant. How my mind did wonder about their early years! Why had Father committed so great a sin against Joan and God? The visiting pastor from Beverly spoke of God's intent in marriage and said, "The woman was made of a rib out of the side of Adam; not made out of his head to top him, nor out of his feet to be trampled upon by him, but out of his side to be equal with him; under his arm to be protected, and near his heart to be beloved."

Can a man who wholeheartedly loves his wife commit the sin of adultery? Did Father love my real mother more fully than Joan? The possibility of my real mother's sweetness and innocence was both perplexing and intriguing, compelling me to know more about her. Perhaps she was already dead, but surely others in the village could bring her to memory if I implored them.

John and I sat near the fire with Charles in the wooden cradle next to us as I screwed up the courage to share my innermost thoughts. John would tell me what he knew if I made him aware of my heartfelt desire to learn from whose womb I came. Surely, I was the only person in Ipswich or maybe even all of New England who did not know the story.

"John, it is a great miracle and blessing to have such a child as Charles who was so perfectly knit by God in my womb, is it not?"

"You say that each day ten times. What do I always say in response? 'Yes, Mehitabel, you have given birth to a most perfect child,'" John said, smiling. "It brings me great joy to see both you and Richard pour your affections onto our son." John's eyes went back to his passage in the Bible. I must push on or lose this moment.

"John, the love I have for Charles often makes me consider my own childhood. I think of you also and your mother and father. You know they are certainly your flesh and blood, and it saddens me that I may go to my grave never to know who my true mother was." The tone of my voice went from one of sweetness to woeful desperation, but I cared not. "I beg you, John, to tell me all you know. Surely, you know some bits of the truth. It is wretched that my mother's name be given only as 'Whore' by Joan." I pleaded and was soon reduced to tears.

John closed the Bible and placed it on the wooden stand. He knelt beside me with one knee bent and grasped my hands to console me. I enjoyed the warm embrace of a loving husband.

"Mehitabel, I have known for many years of the situation with your family. Truth be told, I am sure all of Ipswich, and many beyond, know of your father's sin and Joan's shame. Some with hateful hearts consider it to be God's judgment upon Joan's cold disposition toward your Father even before your birth."

All John revealed was true, but I marveled such a great secret was concealed from only me. My eyes studied our hands clasped together. Surely, God ordained this moment for John to reveal my birth mother.

"Mehitabel, I was but ten years old when this happened, so I was chased away when the gossips' tongues spoke out against your mother and father. Your father's standing in our village has saved you from much of the disgrace usually suffered by a bastard child. Richard suffered the whip and then the more severe lashes from Joan's tongue. Eighteen years of living with a wife's unforgiving and bitter heart. Many in the village fear Joan, and so say nothing. They just listened to her stories of your childhood mischief and failures."

"John, I have known this is true. I understand the ways of gossip and the ways of our congregation. Most are pious and discuss such matters mostly to keep themselves and others from falling into sin. My wish is to know about my real mother—her name, what she looked like, what became of her."

My husband rose to his feet and walked a few steps to gaze upon the crackling embers of the slight fire. John would not look at me. "Mehitabel, I want to tell what you ask of me, but it is not my sin. It is not my secret to reveal. You must pray, my dear wife. God will reveal what you wish to know in His time, not my time." With those final words, John glanced back at me with a compassionate but resolved spirit and went off into our bedchamber for the night.

Such a small request, to know my true mother's name. One word. Only her given name. I must be content because there were some things of which a godly woman should not speak: my father's sin, my true mother's name, and John's abandonment in the colonies. I must conceal these thoughts in my heart. I must pray.

# CHAPTER TWENTY-THREE

"She who plants thorns must never expect to gather roses. I tell you, Constance neglects those poor children and her husband just as she has neglected her responsibilities to this group of women," Elizabeth exclaimed.

Weary of our chore, some of the women strayed into gossip. Our fingers were numb and stinging, and our backs tired from hours of spinning. Constance had refused to attend our daily gathering to fulfill her quota of skeins of yarn assigned by the village magistrates, but for us to participate in this idle chatter was a sin.

Perhaps it was best to channel our conversation away from gossip. "Yes," I interrupted. "The pearls of wisdom learned from Mistress Hubbard so long ago have been etched in my heart. God has blessed me abundantly with a rose garden of healthy children. I hope never to scatter thorns in my precious family."

I was thankful the goodwives of Ipswich now included me in their rounds of group chores. The church accepted me two years ago as a full, confessing member. Charles, Sarah, and Little John brought us such joy as we raised them in God's will, and we did not spare correction as God's Word cautions parents. Our three children were all below eight years of age. Now all could see that I was with child again.

"Mehitabel, when is this next child expected?" Elizabeth asked.

"Sometime in December unless this one arrives as the last, a bit early," I replied.

"I expect you will call upon me again as the midwife," said Heseda.

Elizabeth, with her foolish tongue, asked, "Your mother, Joan, does not attend you?"

"Why would Mehitabel ask a barren woman to attend her children's birth?" Heseda replied, keeping a sure eye on the spindle. "Besides, Joan is not to be trusted with even the animals. Goody Lawson had a quarrel with her, and a week later she saw Joan point to a neighbor's cow. That heifer died while birthing its calf. Neither lived."

"Don't worry, Heseda," Elizabeth said. "Mehitabel would never let Joan Braybrooke near her during her child's birth, especially now that we have heard Joan is not to be trusted."

*Is Heseda accusing Joan of conjuring up evil spirits?* This was my first hearing of Joan casting a spell upon a poor animal. *Were there other instances of Joan cavorting with Satan's minions? Had Joan evolved from a bitter woman into one who wrote in the Devil's book?*

My chest tightened, and my fingers fumbled with the yarn. *Please, let no one ask if I agreed with Heseda.* "Let's count the skeins to see how many more we need for today," I stammered. *Please, God, let this story be false.*

Our lives with three children knew hard work and sleepless nights, but every day I was reminded we were in a season of blessing. John was a diligent farmer, and we shared in Father's prosperity. Father's affection for John grew, and John could not have been a truer son in return.

Father took it upon himself to instruct young Charles to read. He hoped Charles would grow to be a learned young man. With God's blessing, we all hoped he might someday attend the college where the sons of our prosperous men studied. Father's wish was for all his grandsons to be learned men—either ministers of God's Word or lawyers.

Thinking back to the time when Charles was in my womb, I recalled little desire for food and no strength for my daily chores. Now I smiled at those memories and knew the luxury of rest was no longer mine. Being the mother of three young ones gave me no opportunity to consider my own needs. I pressed on and tended to my garden of roses, knowing my discomforts would soon pass.

The harvest was good, the best we had known. Our prosperity dampened when new sojourners came from the motherland. The floodgates opened again in England because of the Great Fire of London and fear of plague, and the newcomers thought they would gain sizeable plots of land as soon as they stepped off their ships. They did not realize each acre of fertile land was acquired only through toil, hardships, and our good fortune as early settlers. Newly opened lands would not be theirs until the constant battles with the native people ended.

As daylight grew longer in June, the dark mood of the people of Ipswich mixed with the overwhelming summer heat. Elizabeth rushed to greet me with the latest news her husband overheard at the tavern. "Goody Downing, have you heard of the savages' uprising just south of Kennebunk? We met a young woman who escaped with her children before the natives could capture them. The heathens walked right into her home. They'd been scouting the area and knew most men were away fighting further up north."

Stories such as these were repeated again and again, as King Phillip's War between the Indians and colonists consumed everyone's thoughts. The light of day faintly lifted our spirits, but the dark of night blanketed our village with anxiety and nightmares.

The dangers we experienced in the colony's early years were far greater now. There was no escape from the frightening discussions and plans. I dreaded the thought of John going off again to fight against the Indians. He had returned just weeks before from his last adventure. John remained safe only through God's protection.

Mr. John Endicott sought to bring God's Word to the native people. A significant number were known to be praying Indians, but many in New England did not know who to trust among the praying natives. Reverend Hubbard often spoke with great caution and alarm about them. His words did nothing to give us hope of an easy peace. Our church members fasted and prayed at Reverend Hubbard's advice, and we begged our great and mighty God to let this dread pass over us.

It was not to be.

After the children were asleep, John sat by the fire, and I rested in a chair nearby. He turned his head toward me and said, "Mehitabel, we need to talk again about my joining up with Samuel Appleton's men in Boston. It is my duty to give support in the uprising. There is word the Narragansett tribe has given assistance to Metacomet."

John's announcement gave me dread. I knew I must trust it as God's will for New England to be a holy place where His Word would reign supreme. Still, my husband's words ran through me like the pierce of a savage's arrow.

"John, I know you must go. The children and I shall stay with Father and Mother while you are away." That John would leave again overpowered my desire to remain calm. "When must you go? Our child will arrive before the new year comes." My voice quivered with the flow of a steady stream of tears. A woman meeting her time of travail must not be a worry to a man serving a greater master, but I could not contain my deep emotions and intense fears.

John knelt on the floor beside me and took my hands in his. "Mehitabel, you will be safe, and I promise to return to you just as I have in the past."

I breathed deeply and knew I must stay strong to give John reassurance. "I promise we will remain close to Father's home to cause you no worry." With these words and a long embrace, we began to prepare and prayed for our safety.

In early December, John departed with Major Samuel Appleton to meet up in Dedham with five hundred twenty-seven members of the Massachusetts militia. Governor Josiah Winslow of Plymouth Colony was named Commander-in-Chief, and Appleton's men joined with hundreds from Plymouth and Connecticut. One hundred fifty Mohegan warriors would also engage in the battle against their longtime foe, the Narragansett Indians.

These days of December were amongst the most bitter we could recall when winter was in its youth. At night, I wondered about John's suffering, his sacrifice, and his concern for us. My life would be far more wretched than it once was if John should perish. One bullet or arrow would give my family need to return to my father's house permanently—the house of my childhood tribulations and pain. My children should never suffer their grandmother's cold hands and heart.

My David was born during this terrible time of fighting. John and I had chosen his name to honor the mighty king of Israel, and we trusted God would also carry us through the horrors of wars and treacherous times. *May my son never have the need to go to battle as did his father!*

It was the first day of the new season when the door flew open, and a servant's voice called out, "Goody Downing, you must come to the meetinghouse. A rider has arrived with a letter for all to hear."

Father and I rushed out into the crisp air to head for the gathering place, but neither of us could make haste. I was still recovering from David's birth, and Father's leg caused him to hobble on the muddy path.

A rider dispatched from the camp gave us the names of the fallen, but there was no report of injuries. Though I was grateful John's name was not read aloud, I was vigilant not to show excessive happiness. It would be a great insensitivity to rejoice that my John would return while others dealt with sorrow for their dead.

"Governor Winslow's brave men launched a strike on the Narragansett to catch them by surprise and captured the Narragansett Fort on December 19," announced the rider. "Major Samuel Appleton and his remaining forces are now in Boston and will soon return. It was a great victory our Almighty God ordained for His people."

The snow and winds stayed steady during the following days. In early January, a great rabble of noise could be heard throughout Ipswich signaling Major Appleton's troops' return. I sat by David's cradle but jumped to my feet to gather the other children to greet their father. The shouts outside surely meant John was returning to us.

The neighing of his exhausted horse announced John's arrival. As he came through the doorway, he quickly placed his musket in the corner so he could receive his loved ones in his arms. His short, limping walk told me all was not well, but his arms were still strong, and his face unblemished. As he bent over to embrace the children, a grimace of pain made it obvious John had indeed been wounded.

"Ah, my family. It is a blessing and God's great mercy that I am home." His arms seemed able to embrace all three children at one time. Their joy was as if the children and John were in the fields tumbling about in midsummer. He stumbled backward and fell to the ground but quickly rose to his feet. John clenched his teeth to hide his pain.

David did not need us to announce his presence. The commotion and squeals of happiness from his brothers and sister were enough to wake him. He greeted his father with a loud wail. I gathered up our son and brought him to John. "Welcome home. John, this is David, and Father and Mother have helped care for him." It was right to give honor to Joan. Perhaps our time living with them this past month might soothe the years of discontent.

Charles chirped in, "Grandfather calls him King David. Do you know of the story of King David, Father?" We all laughed at our boy's sweet innocence, and John replied it was a fitting name for our young ruler.

Father signaled for a servant to put the horse in the barn so we might all sit and hear of John's great adventures. Mother fetched a mug of warm rum when she saw John needed warmth and care.

John embraced the children for some time and asked them many questions. "Charles, have you new verses to recite for me tonight? Sarah, have you been learning to care for our new little king? Jack, have you been a good boy for your mother and grandparents?" And so his questioning went, and then he asked the servants to provide the children a sweet delicacy away from us. They should not hear reports about the Indian wars.

Father began the query. "John, we have received word God bestowed great success upon Winslow's men. Tell us what you can."

John lifted his mug, enjoyed a hefty sip of warm rum, and sighed. He sat up in his chair a bit straighter and spoke with pride. "Major Appleton assured the men our fighting was valiant, and we achieved a great victory. He received word of the positions of the Narragansett, and we gave them a great surprise in the vast swamp near Rhode Island where the Indians laid in wait. Our men learned the skills of warfare practices in the forests. Our numbers, powerful cannons, and weapons outmatched our enemy."

Father interrupted as he always marked victory with numbers. "John, are there yet reports to be made of the dead and injured, both of the English and the heathen?"

"Of the totals, I am not sure, but our dead and wounded totaled not many over one hundred. The Indians suffered many hundreds of losses, and there are reports of retreat and regrouping. Major Appleton is confident the Indians suffered a significant defeat, and we may be near the end of such hostilities. His belief of this is persuasive, and he has resigned his command and intends to live out his years here in Ipswich, just as I do."

I began to help remove John's boots but stopped as his pain increased. "Husband, our prayers have been answered. I can tell that you look in good health, but your feet and legs show me all is not well."

"Wife, God indeed protected me from the bullets and arrows of the Indians, but most men suffered the harshness of the snow with little relief. My feet and legs were like stinging stones as I walked through the frozen waters of the swamp. At times I feared I could not go a step further so great was the pain. I am home now and have thought much about the healing wisdom of my mother-in-law. Joan, have you some medicines or poultice to assist my healing?"

Joan jumped to her feet to consider what healing herbs and remedies she would use. It wasn't long before she returned with a soothing poultice of dried mullein flowers mixed with oils. As our patriarch, Father called upon God's healing power with praise and thanksgiving. While Joan tended to John's wounds, Father lifted his hands and praised Almighty God for John's safe return and the great victory over the Indians.

As Richard and Joan finished their tasks, John took a deep sigh and asked Joan for more warm rum, but this time he requested she fill his cup to the brim.

# Chapter Twenty-Four

John's legs and feet were frightful to behold as his weeks of misery wore on. Father insisted we continue to stay with them so Mother could be diligent in John's care. Her first remedy was to have a servant hunt a young rabbit and kill it outside. She placed the rabbit in a bowl on the floor and cut it open. John's right foot, the most severely affected, was placed inside the carcass, and the warm blood bathed his sores and white skin.

Joan regularly made a poultice of cold mashed onion and applied it twice a day to the affected areas. As his wounds began to heal, John nursed the pain with warm rum, consuming more and more each day. Father cautioned John to consider moderation in drink, but Mother assured him that John soon would not need to consume so great an amount. John's drinking was not just for his discomfort but also for what he witnessed in battle with the savages. Most painful were memories of his close friends' deaths in the skirmishes.

We continued to receive periodic reports of small excitements, but word finally came back that the New England forces had defeated the Indians. This news gave us assurance the colonies might soon enter a time of peace and prosperity without the need for our constant vigilance against the native populations.

With the spring planting at hand, John and Father joined my dowry land with those belonging to Father.

"My grandchildren will someday consider both these farms their own. For now, we must take into account their stomachs. Four little ones indeed need much." Father wished no harm to come to those he loved, but John's excessive drinking was of increasing concern.

God's hand was upon our crops, and midsummer promised a bountiful harvest. Father hired the Hobart brothers to assist in the harvest. Their dead father foolishly willed the house and all his lands to his very young new wife. She soon remarried and left his sons with no lands or inheritance. Father testified in court on their behalf, but the will was solid, leaving no doubt their father had been a fool.

Eventually, John and I moved back into our own home located just across the stream from Father's. Both households enjoyed great benefits from the brothers' misfortune, but unfortunately, they were a bitter source of contention. They became John's good fellows, accompanying him to the ordinary where the servants and other villagers often gathered in the evenings for drink and games.

Each night was the same. I was left alone at home wondering if my husband was drifting down the road in lockstep with the Devil. When he returned, John's drunken voice and footsteps would sound even before the door opened. In haste, I would grab young David and nurse him so I would not suffer John's foul temper. John would utter words of disgust when he saw the babe in my arms, but then he would soon be asleep.

I did not disapprove of the rum but of the company John kept and his excesses. I prayed our good minister might preach of the clear sin of drunkenness, and God soon spoke through Reverend Hubbard. The sermon I hoped for came from the book of Isaiah. As he preached, the reverend's eyes searched for those who had need to hear. He clenched the lectern with his fists, and his body thrust forward as he declared, "Woe to those who rise early in the morning that they may run after strong drink, who tarry late into the evening as wine inflames them!"

I gave thanks for so pertinent a message from the Holy Scriptures and considered it timely to bring up the verses with John that evening. He sat in his chair and gazed at the embers as if in a trance until my words shattered his vacant stare.

"John, did you not feel God's Holy Spirit talking to you from the book of Isaiah today? Husband, I fear the great Devil himself takes over when you share much rum and heavy liquors with the servants. You are in covenant with the Holy Church, and yet you defy the words instructing us to live blameless and upright lives."

John's solemn expression did not change. He walked to the hearth, set a new log upon the embers, and muttered, "Wife, consider your past sins before you bring judgment down on me."

"John, I have given examination of the state of my soul, and assuredly know I am forgiven. Husband, these reprobate practices have stained your walk before the Lord."

John stood for just a moment and glared at me. "Consider Proverbs tells us to *Give strong drink unto him that is ready to perish, and wine unto those that be of heavy hearts. Let him drink, and forget his poverty, and remember his misery no more.* God speaks of people such as my friends and me in these words. Mehitabel, speak no more of this!"

# CHAPTER TWENTY-FIVE

In April of 1679, we received word that John's mother, Lucy Winthrop Downing, passed away at George's illustrious London home. The news first reached the ears of the most influential men in Ipswich. Words of consolation for John were embedded in praises for such a noble and godly woman. Villagers remembered Lucy as an excellent example of a Puritan mother whose greatest accomplishment was to have raised a learned and decorated son such as George. The townsfolk never gave mention to the fact that John was long ago cast aside by Lucy as she pursued an exalted legacy for her eldest son.

Shades of darkness were ever present in the year that followed Lucy Downing's death. While our prosperity grew, Satan became unleashed in our home with his cunning ways, although John no longer spent his evenings at the ordinary with friends. The righteous people of the village were obliged to keep an eye on their neighbors, and tongues began to wag about the great supply of liquors that made their way to our home.

By day, John presented himself as an industrious man who walked about Ipswich with his head held high. By night, as I gathered my roses for our nightly prayers, John sat by the fire with a distant, blank expression. Heavy spirits would soon squelch the fire in his soul. It became clear John was a great pretender of God's Word and constraints.

Reverend Hubbard came to our home one evening in mid-July, just before sunset. With him was Goodman Smith, a deacon of the church. They likely suspected to find John at home in a reclusive state after a day of heavy toil in the fields.

I invited them to come in. "John is with the animals in the barn and will join us soon."

Goodman Smith walked through our home, taking liberties by opening the cabinets and sniffing for any telling aromas. The purpose of their visit was clear.

Reverend Hubbard sat with me in his usual dignified manner at the table. "Mehitabel, we come as friends to you both, but I also come as your minister given charge your salvation. Word of John's cloistered imbibement has fallen upon the church and town council. I come with Goodman Smith to plead John's case before Almighty God. We pray God prompts John to turn away from the excesses of drinking for the sake of his soul." Reverend Hubbard spoke in a kind, yet resolute manner.

"I assure you, Reverend, John is a good father, a loving husband, and a good provider. We seek to follow God's holy edicts and direction. Since the birth of our son, John only drinks when Mother's remedies provide no relief. Even the Apostle Paul encouraged Timothy to drink wine for his stomach ailments. John believes he lives within the boundaries of Holy Scripture."

As he strode through the entrance, John nodded a customary greeting, not surprised to see the Reverend and Mr. Smith. The two visitors sat with stiff postures and serious expressions. John joined them at the table and uttered not a word. His indiscretions were no longer secret.

"John, Reverend Hubbard and Goodman Smith come to our home as God's representatives to speak of their concerns for us." Hoping not to be drawn into the upcoming chastisement, I found a reason to leave the room. "I will fetch some cool teas for you and our guests."

I went to the kitchen and found a few of our servants huddled together near the door as they pretended to be at task. "Go to your rooms and leave Mr. Downing and me alone with our guests. I caution you to be discreet. You will be met by the lash if you speak to anyone of this visit!"

Rarely harsh with the servants, I hoped to trust their loyalty with what they heard and observed while in our service. It was apparent that the village authorities might have used their influence with the servants to secure information about our lives.

When I returned, the conversation had already turned to Scripture passages and prayers for John's repentance. He was entreated to forsake all temptations. Reverend Hubbard ended with a passage of Scripture seared into his memory, *Know ye not that the unrighteous shall not inherit the kingdom of God? Be not deceived: neither fornicators, nor idolaters, nor adulterers, nor effeminate, nor abusers of themselves with mankind, nor thieves, nor covetous, nor drunkards, nor revilers, nor extortioners, shall inherit the kingdom of God.*

Reverend Hubbard stood in the middle of the room, raised his hands toward heaven and invoked God's mercy through prayer.

John sat motionless with just an occasional heavy sigh, having been chastised not only by mere mortal men but also by God Almighty. "Sirs, I have been humbled and properly humiliated in accordance with God's Word. I give you my word as God's holy servant: I will no longer give in to temptation, nor will I be the cause of others to stumble, for that is my duty as a child of God. I thank you both for your concern for my very soul and salvation," John spoke in a solemn and contrite manner.

Reverend Hubbard and Mr. Smith stood and appeared to accept John's confession and humility. As abiding Puritans, they were not yet ready to end the matter. "John, we will pray for you. Both of us will pay more visits such as this to witness your true repentance. Know that Satan stands at this door and bids you join him. Heed God's Word, John!"

Reverend Hubbard and Mr. Smith left with the same somberness in which they entered, as Reverend Hubbard uttered his parting words. "Good night to you, and may God bestow mercy and kindness on you both."

When our guests departed, John returned to his chair to sip the tea and then brought the Bible to his lap. For many minutes, John silently pondered as he read, his left hand firm against his forehead. "Mehitabel, come and sit next to me. Here is the passage I shall now hold dearest to my heart."

John's finger followed under each word as he read, "Mehitabel, hear, for this is God's Word: *It is good neither to eat flesh, nor to drink wine, nor any thing whereby thy brother stumbleth, or is offended, or is made weak.* Those are the words I will pray to live by for my family's sake. For *your* sake, my wife."

John fixed his chilly gaze upon me. "For your sake; for you, Mehitabel, I will not continue to stumble."

John's words hung in the air like a dense, oppressive fog. At that moment, my secret sin was unmasked and laid bare. The good men of the town suspected my husband to be the indulgent consumer of Satan's brew. What was not unveiled to our minister was my growing affection for rum used to wash away my fears and shame. My covert sin was now exposed. During his chastisement, my husband also sought to shield me from the blame and humiliation.

# Chapter Twenty-Six

Cascading waterfalls of melancholy overwhelmed me. If not for the numbing comfort of my rum, I sometimes despaired I might drown. The billows and waves tossed me to and fro in a roar calling out from the depths of my soul. In the light of day, I sensed God's loving hand. His affirmations told me I was raising my children according to His edicts. At night, the truth of my sins washed over me.

Dread of the return of the savages and the howls of the wolves in the dense forest so near wore down my mind and soul. John's vow to turn away from our shared nocturnal wicked pleasure left me alone in humiliation. My childhood shame returned, and I sank deeper and deeper into the melancholy that had been my partner long ago. I prayed to go into the evening with a smile upon my face, but my soul remained unconsoled. Why must my life be so dispirited with tears that flowed endlessly into the night?

My family's lives entered a new season. No longer was I the young mother required to tend only to her household and children. My father was advancing in years and needed more from John and me. How I desired to return his many kindnesses and love, and this aspiration should have strengthened me. Instead, I feared I would disappoint Father, and the possibility I would dishonor him struck an irrational fear in my heart.

Father's legs were a source of significant pain as of late. He never gave much heed to physical discomfort. When his worn knee slipped out of joint, he pounded it back in place with a wooden mallet. Father sought to ward off the pain and trembling in his hands, but not because he feared the discomfort. His life's work came through his hands. What use were his feet if he could no longer walk to his fields? What good would his gnarly fingers be if he could not embrace his grandchildren and build toys for them?

"Mehitabel, bring my walking sticks to me so I can assist John in the barn with the calving. There is a good stool there where I may sit. I shall give John instruction if that beast gives us difficulties with her coarse disposition."

I tried to convince Father that John had a good understanding of animal husbandry and would not need help. "Father, do you not fear those old legs will go beneath you if you do not take better care and rest?" I scolded him but knew my words would have no effect.

"Dear daughter, these old legs have not yet failed me, and they won't fail the old beast or John," was Father's reply.

I shook my head in wonder at his steadfast determination and dedication to those he so loved. The anticipation of him no longer being with us was a great sadness I bore. He would someday be called to his reward in heaven, but for now, Father was my rock here on earth. These thoughts rushed over me whenever I saw his struggles with the curse of a withering body.

As the harvest came into its fullest and busiest of times, Father's visits to our home became scarcer and scarcer. Mother attended to him with her ointments and teas, but we all knew his soul would soon be among the ages.

Dr. Bennett examined Father for his heart palpitations, but Mother assured him her herbs were the best remedy. As his breathing became labored and strained, Father took to his bed, and there he remained. I visited him each morning and brought the children to comfort him. He took most pleasure in their Scripture recitations and childlike comments.

After Sabbath services one morning, the children and I walked down the path for our daily visit. Father's solitude was interrupted by the whirlwind of four children running into their beloved grandfather's room.

David sat at the end of his bed. "Grandfather, Charles and I have been praying for you to be well again for the rides on your shoulders this spring. Mother says I may soon be big enough to carry you upon my shoulders."

With such sweet hopes and words, Father smiled but then began to cough violently. He needed another dose of black pepper and honey tea.

"Children, go in the next room so I may help Grandfather gain his strength. Then we can all listen to your new verses, and you can tell him of Reverend Hubbard's message from this morning." I was proud my young ones obediently left the room as they clung to the joyful hope of better days with their grandfather.

"Mehitabel, indeed your garden of roses is blooming. Who would have expected so great a treasure grandchildren would become?" Father sighed deeply to gain the strength to continue. "It brings such pleasure to my heart that God has blessed our family so abundantly through you and John. You, my child, have always been my dearest gift from God." Father laid his head back on the downy pillow and gazed at the oak beams above him.

He then turned his eyes upon me and reached out for me to sit next to him. "My dear one, I know I have committed sins and treacheries against God that have brought many burdens to you since you were born. I beg your forgiveness. You, Mehitabel, have proven our God is indeed the bestower of great mercies, forgiveness, and restoration. In you, I have seen that God can use all things for His glory and our good."

I gazed at his face, and at that moment sensed these would be our parting words. Father must have also known this was his final chance to bestow his blessing on my life. I buried my head in his linens and held his withered hands in mine. He closed his eyes to restore his strength.

Father's lips trembled, and his dark lashes brimmed heavy with tears. His eyes opened, and a lone tear traced down his wrinkled cheek. "Mehitabel, I have prayed for your forgiveness, but there continues to be a deep hole in your spirit. Joan has not been the mother you needed, but forgive her as my sin hurt her and crushed her spirit. She has done her best."

Father's words became more labored, and he paused to receive divine help to complete his final words. "Mehitabel, I made Joan a promise I would never reveal the name of your real mother, but please inform Mistress Hubbard and our good minister that after my death, they may tell you her name. I wish nothing more than for your spirit to be at rest in God's peace and grace. You must promise to completely forgive your mother just as God has forgiven you, my dear Mehitabel."

I wanted nothing more than to give my father peace as his body and spirit lingered just a while longer. My head nodded as I whispered into his ear, "Yes, I promise."

I reached out to Father and held his hand. His eyes closed and did not open again. The vein in his neck throbbed slowly, and it seemed to be the only movement in the room. My eyes became fixed on the steady beat. Then, the pulsing in the vein ceased. My eyes continued to stay fixed as I searched for any motion. Father's heart had beaten its last time. My Father in heaven allowed us to profess our final words as He knew we should. I escorted my earthly father into heaven just as both of my fathers would have wanted.

# Chapter Twenty-Seven

The tolling of the bell echoed in late November as the people of our village came together for the solemn procession to Father's final resting place. The ringing told of the finality of Father's many years. All who knew him gathered at his house, walked to his grave, and stood near as Father was lowered into the ground. The minister read no words, and no sermon was delivered, as was our custom in New England. Family and friends said their final goodbyes without a word. Only gentle sobs rippled through the crowd of mourners.

We proceeded to the meetinghouse for solemn prayers to grieve for the loss of my father. Reverend Hubbard walked beside me, only speaking as we entered the door. "Mehitabel, your father was amongst the first in Ipswich, and he shall be missed. It has been a good thing to see a man so convinced of his depravities and so eager for God's forgiveness. Richard was an excellent father to you, Mehitabel. Your grief must be heavy."

I could only nod my head in agreement, for to speak of Father, even with affection, was overwhelming. I could not end a sentence without my voice quavering. I desperately wanted to ask Reverend Hubbard to break his silence about my mother, but this was not the proper time.

"Mehitabel, know Mistress Hubbard deeply regrets not being able to come today to give you comfort. My wife is being tended by the doctors as we speak. She asked I convey her wish for you to visit so she can read comforting words of Scripture and mourn with you."

"Reverend, I know your dear wife has been ailing, as she has not been seen about since the autumn chill has set upon our village. My care for Father has overwhelmed me, and I have been errant in my responsibilities to your good wife. Please tell her I am humbled and grateful to have you both as my godly influencers. You kept both John and me on God's path when we were on the road to perdition. I shall visit Mistress Hubbard soon."

That evening, John made sure the servants tended to the children so I could sit with him to study the Scriptures. He chose from the gospel of John. *Do not let your hearts be troubled. Ye believe in God; believe also in me. My Father's house has many rooms; if that were not so, would I have told ye that I am going there to prepare a place for thee? And if I go and prepare a place for thee, I will come back and take ye to be with me that ye also may be where I am.*

John stopped and smiled. "Mehitabel, I believe your father is with the saints. They are building a room for you and me to be next to him there in heaven."

I knelt before John with my head in his lap. "John, Father's last moments with me were a precious gift, giving me surety of his love. He promised that Reverend and Mistress Hubbard would reveal my birth mother's name after his death." I stared intently into his eyes. "I know you also have the power to give me this desire of my heart. John, will you grant me this?"

"Mehitabel, I know these may have been your father's words as he lay on his deathbed, but he and I also spoke of this promise when you and I first married. Richard made it clear that no one was to disclose your real mother's name until after Joan's death, or if she remarried. You shall need to be patient as your request shall not be granted until one of the two has taken place. We must consider Widow Braybrooke's sorrow to be just as great as yours."

"Father made no reference to these conditions when he gave this promise!" My face became rigid, and my jaw clamped tight.

"No further words will be spoken, Mehitabel. Our good minister has agreed to this."

I wanted to run out of the house before I said anything I might regret. John retired to bed, but I sat alone before the crackling fires and nursed my disappointment and bitterness with rum. It was the only friend that understood the woe and anguish in my soul. As I drank the last warm sip, my mind became inflamed with the thought of John's authority as my husband. He could not be challenged, but I was determined to visit Reverend Hubbard as soon as possible.

Groggified, I drifted to sleep in the chair until the next morning when Hannah found me slumped on the cold floor. She understood my melancholy and woke me before John or the children stirred. My dear Hannah.

The following week, I prepared fruited bread, cheese, and pottage to bring to my dear Mistress Hubbard. Another layer of snow blanketed the village, and so Peter readied the horse for our wintery ride to our parson's house. I wanted to appear as though concern for her was the only motivation for my visit. Perhaps she might take mercy on me and grant the one thing I wanted to know most on this earth.

A serving girl led me into the grand parlor which invoked reminisces of myself as a child seated at Mistress Hubbard's feet. The familiar pictures, rugs, china, and memories of Scripture lessons swept over me as I recalled those tender moments.

Mistress Hubbard appeared at the parlor entrance with servants on each side. They lowered her carefully into a chair, and the dear woman smiled before she began to speak in her typical sweet manner. "Mehitabel, it is so good to see you. I know my husband shared my sadness about your father's passing, but Richard has gone to his reward. Such is our life here on earth; how quickly we move from birth to death."

"Thank you for your many kindnesses. I received your letter sharing your thoughts and Scriptures. They have been a balm for my heart."

"Oh, Mehitabel, I hope you have asked for God to give you strength to fully forgive your father and your mother, too. Joan grieves and needs her family during these days. She seems to be so alone these weeks."

My words thus far had not included any thoughts of Joan's needs. She had shut herself off from us, save a few words and requests for only John. That I had no desire to ever again be in Joan's presence was not something to divulge to so compassionate a woman as Margaret Hubbard.

"I have made attempts to bring her consolation, but Mother has chosen to be closed up in their ... I mean her house alone." After just a moment's silence, I added, "This has been Joan's pattern as long as I have known her. We have never had a true mother and daughter relationship. None at all."

"Yes, what you speak of is true. I hope God continues to minister to her soul concerning her bitterness spilled out onto you, the innocent one. Mehitabel, I ask that you go before God and petition Him for the gift of forgiveness and mercy for Joan. There is no other way, my child."

I should have expected Mistress Hubbard to express such compassion, but not even she understood the depths of my bitterness against Joan. Calling Joan "Mother" now stirred up the resentment I had been forced to carry for so many years.

"Mistress Hubbard, I will be able to forgive Joan's wrath and offenses only when I learn the name of my birth mother. Father promised me on his deathbed that you would tell me. I assure you it is only her name I seek and need no knowledge of the details of my father's sin. I simply wish to know my mother's name."

Surely, Mistress Hubbard would perceive my voice only as sincere and anguished and would be merciful. Tears puddled in my eyes.

"Mehitabel, your father spoke to us many years ago because he knew you would request to know about your birth mother. At present, I must honor your father's wish and can only tell you she is still living and is a godly woman, but Mehitabel—God desires for you to come with a merciful and forgiving heart. His generosity must refuse some requests. At times, it is a greater kindness to withhold rather than to bestow. You shall see in due course what I say is true."

Beyond disappointed, I left the Hubbards' home feeling disheartened and sullen. It could not be God's will to thwart such a natural inclination to know my beginnings. The desire to know the name of my true mother was as sensible as hearing the stories of my grandparents and all my ancestors from Father's family. I sought to live by God's commandments and holy decrees and raise my children to honor Him. Mistress Hubbard was wrong. There could be no reason for this secret to continue. Perhaps only I understood God's will and true desires.

# CHAPTER TWENTY-EIGHT

There was nothing left to feel, nothing left to say as I departed the Hubbards' home. I was hurt, disappointed, and mostly angry that Mistress Hubbard supposed it best that I wait. Wait for Joan to be in better spirits? How dare anyone presume they thought it best I wait for God's timing! Why would God want to hide a person's name anyway?

Peter offered his hand as I climbed onto the carriage for our journey. He caught me when I stumbled over my skirt, and then I fumbled onto the hard bench. My red face and pursed lips illuminated my frustration, but I spoke not a word of it to my old friend. As he gathered the reins, Peter paused when he witnessed my tears but seemed mystified as to how to console me.

After just a short while, Peter pulled back on the reins and declared with confidence, "Goodwife, I shall take you to Obadiah Woods' tavern for a short while. You are in need of a warm beverage and food to raise your spirits. I had hoped a visit with Mistress Hubbard would bring you comfort, but I see that did not happen."

When we entered the ordinary, a spirit of discontentment swept over me like the sulky tones of a quarrelsome child. I must be cautious as the tithingmen were always present, but I did not see Goodman Smith. It mattered not since everyone reported the villagers' indiscretions to one another. Any imprudence would reach the tithingmen's ears, but at the moment, my judgment was clouded.

The patrons comforted me with consoling words about my father and offered stories of his goodness and humorous foibles. To be sure, Father perhaps gave far too much concern for the affairs of others. Such was the state of relationships between almost all these people of Ipswich. They were a meddlesome lot, bringing one another to court in matters both large and small, but Father was never deterred in his pursuit of justice. He was so like the early villagers who perceived themselves as more civilized than their countrymen left behind in England who settled most disputes with brawls.

Peter and I sat with good friends and made merry. I told them I had just been to Mistress Hubbard's and reported she was well. It was prudent to pacify any gossip's ear if they assumed I had been idle all day. Peter encouraged me to eat as I had displayed little appetite since my father's death.

Thomas Wells, father's old foe, sat at a distant table with one of his vile and disagreeable kin. I recalled when he brought Father to court years ago, and Thomas' neighbors gave testimony against Father. During the next court session, these same people changed their alliances and spoke ill of Thomas. What goes around comes around.

On our return home, Peter stopped before we arrived at our farm. "Goodwife, know you are welcome to ask for my company any time you wish to go out for a visit. Your countenance is now gay and uplifted."

"Peter, I thank you for your kindness. My heart has indeed brightened." I tottered as I stepped off the carriage. The rum made me more merry than wise.

Hannah greeted me after she took my basket and cape. "Mistress, you must sit and warm by the fire. I have broth and some fresh bread ready. Surely, you are hungry."

I smiled at Hannah, so pleased she now lived with John and me as a servant. "Dear Hannah, Mistress Hubbard fed me well, and we enjoyed the bread. I am quite content and wish to tend to the children's lessons. I fear they have not been diligent in my absence."

Mad as a bull among a swarm of bees, John stormed into the house. After hanging his musket, he settled onto the bench, ready for a fight. He slammed his pouch of documents on the table. "I intended this trip to Boston to be my last and to finally settle your Father's affairs. It started out pleasant with the trip to Harvard College. They were so thankful for your Father's generous donation and assured me Richard's grandsons would one day be welcome. I thought all would proceed well, until Joan arrived."

*Joan. Of course!* Most of our troubles lately centered around Joan's excessive demands. Now I understood John's foul mood.

"She now disputes the western boundary line and the outside buildings of our tenants. Thinks they are hers and wants their rent given to her. I do not understand her. At times she appears amicable, but that is only because I bear the burden of her lands. I am beginning to believe the scandalous stories about her."

"What stories have you heard, John?"

John reached for his hat and walked to the door. "I shouldn't repeat the gossip of others, not even to you."

Did John overhear tales of Joan giving the evil eye or casting a spell upon a neighbor's wandering hogs rooting into her field? So like John to not fall into the sin of gossip.

John's encounters with Joan likely reminded him that Father's gift of dowry lands was the reason he prospered as a farmer. Both of our mothers had disappointed him. John's mother distributed the Downing lands to distant Winthrop relations deemed more worthy than Emanuel's own sons. Lucy's betrayal ate away at his usually tolerant attitude. Even after death, her legacy stung of disdain for anyone less than nobility.

In the following weeks, Hannah was a great friend, often accompanying me on my increasingly frequent visits to the ordinary. I did not fear the scandalous tongues of Ipswich with Hannah at my side. She was careful to keep my gut plied with food to withstand the frivolous drinks I consumed. It gave the appearance of such a good plan, and I was able to perform all the chores and duties of a wife and mother while still making merry with dear friends at the ordinary. John was not ignorant of my visits, but there was no reason for concern as long as I brought no shame with unseemly behavior.

All this changed when John and I received a summons from the courts during the early planting season in 1684. John assumed the matter at hand was a legal one concerning another property boundary issue. We entered the courtroom the next morning, uncertain of the cause for our summons. Five austere men sat behind the bench, and John Appleton prayed for wisdom and justice for all those summoned.

There sat Goodman Giddens, the new tithingman assigned to our family. Giddens was a slight man of middle age who performed his job with excessive eagerness to prove himself worthy of his new position. He would pace back and forth near the doors of the taverns in Ipswich each night. It seemed he was at every ordinary seven days a week. Perhaps there must be more than one of him who wandered the roads in search of indiscreet behaviors. Might I be the first villager listed on his monthly report?

Giddens handed Abraham Perkins his list of accusations. Now there was another person to dread! Abraham's appointment on the town court was surely dire news for John and me as his bitterness toward me had lingered since the fire. His son Jacob's newly built house was struck by lightning just a few years after the fire I was accused of setting in my youth. God must have sent those punishing strikes with His very hands. The fire happened on the Sabbath, and that alone was proof of my vindication, at least in my mind. Now, my enemy held my family's fate in his influential hands.

John and I sat on the front bench with our heads bowed and spoke not a word until summoned by John Wainwright.

"Mehitabel Downing, wife of John Downing of Ipswich, you are accused of public drunkenness on September 15, as you walked from Obadiah Woods' ordinary," Wainwright said. "This accusation was submitted by Samuel Giddens to the court. What say you, Goody Downing?"

John held his hand up to ward off these allegations. "Your honors, our loyal servants always accompany my wife and have assured me Mehitabel shows prudence and does not imbibe in excess."

"John Downing, Mr. Giddens observed Goody Downing's excesses and not just this one time. He suspects she has behaved improperly on many occasions. The court will leave the discipline to you, sir, since this is Mehitabel's first offense."

Abraham Perkins peered down from his lofty bench and folded his arms across his chest and bellowed so all could hear, "This is not Mehitabel's first appearance in front of the Ipswich Court. Master Wainwright, you may not be aware that Mehitabel was in court for arson sixteen years ago. Mehitabel, fast and pray to God that your reprehensible behaviors cease. Bring no further shame and discredit to your family, your husband, and your father's memory. Think upon the good name of your father, Richard Braybrooke." Abraham then leaned forward and stared down at me as he callously declared, "If he were alive, your father would regret his shameful daughter's indiscretions."

Those words stung like salt on a person's wounds. Bile rose from my innards. I detested Abraham Perkins' arrogance. How dare he invoke my father's name to bring more shame upon me! Bitterness was upon my lips, but I dared not speak to bring yet further disgrace to my husband. My only gratitude was that I was not publicly humiliated in the stocks or put upon the post. My children would have been forced to watch their mother's whipping.

John and I spoke not a word until we arrived near the doorpost of our home. As I began to enter, he grabbed me by the arm with force and eyes that appeared to be on fire. "Mehitabel, I shall call upon the Lord our God to ask Him what to do about this matter, lest my fury be aroused upon you in an ungodly way. I shall consider!"

With those words, he slammed the door behind me. I stood alone outside, then sat on the step and sobbed. John's angry words to Hannah and Peter thundered inside throughout the house, and I regretted they would receive punishment for my sin. I ran into the barn much the same as I did years before when I falsely accused John Beare. I sank into the hay, foul as it was, and stayed the entire night with the animals.

# Chapter Twenty-Nine

A dark cloud descended on my family during these months. Everyone seemed to be in mourning as if a funeral pall was thrown over our home. The windows were dull and gray, and the fires simmered with a sullen glow. Dreariness whispered that there was no point in praying.

John and I were in a season of separation of our affections for one another. We rarely spoke and hadn't been as man and wife since my accusations. I waited weeks for John's decision of my fate, but no physical punishments were meted out. His silence and glances filled with disdain were far more bitter than a hand or whip.

The servants were merciful and did not seek retribution against me because of their punishments. They knew I had been careful at the ordinary, and no one observed any impropriety, but the testimony of servants on behalf of a sinful mistress carries little weight. For their tender mercies, I was blessed.

Our children never overheard words of harshness between their parents, but the wall between John and me was as massive as the ocean between the shores of Mother England and her colonies. The little ones clung to me to make up for John's disaffections, and I was weary from the weight of motherhood I once bore with gladness. Alone by the hearth, I endured their cries for more of my attention.

With my melancholy came a despondency so deep I often forgot about my basic needs. Hunger no longer signaled me to meals. I sometimes grew faint when I did not recognize my thirst. As I went about town, my unkempt appearance was like a bell that rang each morning to announce that I had given up on life and cared about little.

Our home was continually beset by news that challenged our souls and sometimes our wealth. Mother and John finally agreed to settle their issues over boundaries, details of inheritance property, and our responsibilities for her future. We assured her we would continue to maintain her parts of the farm, but that promise doubled John's burdens and duties.

In late April, John and I left the meetinghouse together but truly alone. Heseda waved her arms to attract my attention. "Mehitabel, you must come and look at the posting of the new banns of marriage."

I traced my finger under the words on the posting:

"The banns of marriage between Thomas Penney, widower of Gloucester, and Joan Braybrooke, widow of Richard of Ipswich. Sunday, April 26 in the year of our Lord 1682 is the first date of posting. If any know cause or just impediment why these two persons should not be joined together in Holy Matrimony, ye are to declare it."

How could Joan keep this news from me? Joan covertly covenanted to Thomas Penney, a man of little land and wealth, and they would marry in May.

"John, do you think anyone in Ipswich would dare to find an objection to Joan's marriage to Thomas Penney?" I asked.

"I only hope a new husband during Joan's old age will finally bring her some peace. Perhaps this marriage will be best for us all. Certainly, it will be a relief for me since the responsibility of her lands will no longer be my burden."

To receive no warning of the impending marriage was just one more way Mother chose to humiliate me. Certainly, I would not be invited to witness the nuptials. Pity this man from Gloucester who likely didn't realize he was marrying a woman who was as nasty and headstrong as a wild boar, with a tongue so sharp it could slice a person in two.

I then felt like a fool! Had I forgotten Father's promise on his dying day? The prospect of Joan's marriage reminded me of Father's permission for me to know my real mother's name. I stepped outside the door of the church to wait for the Hubbards. I would now be permitted to know the name of my mother!

Reverend Hubbard escorted Mistress Hubbard as she walked down the stairs. His loving arms steadied her ever shaky movements. She expressed gratitude when her footing was secure on the flat ground.

"Mistress Hubbard, Reverend, may I walk home with you?"

"Of course, Mehitabel, it would be good to have another arm to steady me." Mistress Hubbard's soft, wrinkled face creased with the gift of smiling easily and the joy of finding goodness in small things. She grinned as she pointed to the budding yellow flowers. "Listen to the crocus sing to us as we walk."

I spared no time to remind them of the promise. "The banns for Thomas Penney and Joan were a surprise to John and me today. We are most happy for her and Thomas also. May they have many years together. But this means I may now learn the name of the woman who gave birth to me, as Father promised."

"Mehitabel, the name you speak of will be just a name to you," said Reverend Hubbard in a somewhat dismissive manner. "Her name is Goody Elyss, and she removed from Ipswich a while ago to marry. I know not where she lives, or even if she is alive, but I will try to find out more. You have never met her, I am sure."

"My husband, I have something to confess to you … and Mehitabel," revealed Mistress Hubbard in a contrite tone, "Let us go inside to have tea so that I might explain."

Reverend Hubbard and I lifted her slight frame step by step until we reached the top of the stairs. We walked into the dining room, and Mistress Hubbard asked me to sit across from her.

Mistress Hubbard fussed with her skirt, gathering up the courage to disclose her story, and then confidently proceeded. "William, you were not told of an event that took place many years ago. I arranged for Goody Elyss to have a meeting with Mehitabel, though Mehitabel was not aware of whom she was. Husband, Mehitabel was a child in despair after the fire—so alone in prison, but I could not visit her. A prison cell is not a place where a minister's wife may go. I sent for Alice Elyss, who of course knew that Mehitabel was her child. I asked her to visit and bring a gift of food from me."

My heart began to race wildly, and for a moment I forgot all else. The gentle woman who brought Mistress Hubbard's gift to me in prison was my mother! I assumed she was a dear friend or a servant in the Hubbards' employ. My wretched situation and my hatred of John Beare and Mother had consumed my thoughts during the weeks before my trial. I hadn't seen the truth. My heart's desire had been right before me while I was in prison so long ago!

Mistress Hubbard continued as tears misted in her eyes. "Alice told me later the gift she delivered was of little consequence compared to the gift of holding her daughter. She thought for certain you would realize she was your mother. To Alice, you were the picture of her youthful self when she was a serving girl in your parents' home."

William Hubbard sat silently with his fingers over his lips and then interrupted. "My dear wife, do you think I was not made aware of this visit? I assure you that not much takes place in Ipswich of which I am not cognizant." His broad smile let us both know he approved of his wife's noble gesture.

"Do you think I shall ever be able to see her again?" I asked.

"Dear, that is something to pray for, but it would not be an easy task to find her. She removed from Ipswich to marry, and I fear she has led a hard life. Women who spend their lives in service often do not have the privilege of good food and care. We can only hope in God's mercy she lives," replied Mistress Hubbard.

All night I held the memory of my mother's visit in my heart. I tried to remember how she appeared. She was so lovely, with eyes that sparkled and wisps of golden hair that peeked from her bonnet. Mistress Hubbard spoke the truth about her difficult life. The lines in Alice's face and her wrinkled hands betrayed a hard life, indeed. *I must convince John that I should find my mother, Alice Elyss!*

A full month had passed since Joan's marriage to Thomas. John met with the magistrate and the Penneys to sign the new deed agreements. Upon his return, he reported Joan was civil, but her pretense was transparent. She wanted her fair share and to be done with us as a family.

"Mehitabel, it would behoove our lives to mend our relations with Joan and Thomas. There is no reason for this frosty air to continue between us. I owe Joan a debt of gratitude for her care when I returned home from battle. She is now sixty-nine and likely has not many years left."

The last six months before Father's death taught me that with old age comes its creaks and frailties and that our lives on earth are short. Mistress Hubbard had implored me to make peace with Joan, but things were so much easier without her in my life. The only benefit would be that a reconciliation might please John and help to heal the rift in our marriage. Joan's new life did not include us, and she now had surly stepchildren with whom to contend. I might even look the better daughter now in contrast to Thomas Penney's vulgar children.

Convinced of my own wisdom, I chose not to tell John that I planned to visit the Penney farm later today. My intentions were to wish Joan much happiness in her new marriage and to reconcile my own. I made a gift of fresh cheeses and molasses bread and placed them in a basket and set off on my foot journey to my childhood home, now Joan and Thomas Penney's farm.

Unexpected dark and oppressive clouds began to appear to the west after just a short distance. The weight of the basket was more than I was accustomed to carrying, and I often needed to rest.

A familiar carriage was approaching from the direction of the Penneys' farm. As it neared, I could see it was Reverend Hubbard. He stopped and greeted me with great courtesy. "Mehitabel, it is good to meet up with you. Mistress Hubbard and I have been much concerned, but you look well, my child. Your step should be lively and quick, but that heavy basket weighs you down."

"Thank you for your kind words, Reverend. Yes, I do have happiness in my heart and am on my way to visit my mother, Joan. I bring this gift to honor her marriage to Thomas Penney. It has been months since Father's death, but she has not found it in her heart to speak with me. In the basket is bread in fashion in Boston."

"God is always pleased to see such a good daughter. I have just come from their home, and they are well. Your kindness should warm her heart. But might I perchance offer you a ride in my carriage instead? Dark clouds and heavy rains will soon descend upon us. You don't have much time, and it might be best to return to your home."

"Thank you, Reverend, but I hope to stay and have a lively talk with Joan. You are correct, though. I should make haste. Good day to you, dear Reverend Hubbard."

Perhaps his visit with them was an omen that God might grant me favor with Joan and our time might be one of grace and reconciliation.

The rains had not yet arrived, but the dark clouds menaced nearby. The cool breeze that usually precedes a storm took hold of my cloak, cracking it like a silken sail, and my bonnet laces danced violently in the wind. I knocked at the familiar door of my childhood home and took in a deep breath. It weighed on my heart that Father's house now belonged to Thomas Penney, but it was Joan who traded her property rights to now be Goody Penney.

I was surprised to see Thomas Penney and not Joan or a servant at the door. "Hello, Goodman Penney, it brings much happiness to John and me to hear of Joan's good health and happiness in her marriage to you. I bring a small gift for her. Is she about the house so that I might give these to her and wish her well?"

Thomas's tall frame towered above me, appearing even larger than usual. The scoff on his face was enough for me to know I was not welcome.

"Mehitabel Downing, Joan has no use for you now. Leave her be. You and your father beset her with a vile curse, and she intends to live out the rest of her days with a man on whom she can count—one who will never sin against her the way your lying father did. What kind of man would commit so great a sin against his young wife and put a curse on her to never conceive her own child?"

These words were familiar, but their sting always tormented my heart. I looked down and turned away as tears welled up in my eyes.

"And you, Mehitabel. Your father, as vile as he was, did not deserve the repulsive daughter you have been since birth and now continue to be. Throw your gifts to the swine, and take care that they do not throw them back at you!"

Like a child just disciplined, I slinked down the steps with trembling legs. I had stepped into my past from twenty years ago, and the bitter memories felt fresh. Thomas' scornful words were the same as Joan's from when I was so young; words that hailed down on me, spoken when no one could come to my rescue.

The dark clouds still loomed in the sky, a dreary backdrop for the unexpected outcome of my attempt to make amends with Joan. Thomas Penney and his children were coarse and vulgar, not deserving of even the likes of Joan Braybrooke, though all of his hateful words probably came from her mouth. I now was the foolish person described by so many people in my past.

Why I turned to look back at my childhood home, I will never understand. There stood Joan next to her husband, likely rejoicing in my humiliation. It must have given them great amusement to watch me stumble down the path from their house, my shoulders hunched and spirit broken.

As I rambled down the road near the Cogswells' farm, I stopped and stared at the nearby hogs' pen. Perhaps the swine might indeed enjoy my bread and cheese. They would not choke and die from my food as maybe Joan feared she would if she tasted my gifts. I was determined to have the final vindication and would give the food intended for her to the swine instead. As I stood over the hogs, I unwrapped the loaves of bread so lovingly made and threw them to the animals in a posture of defiance.

"If you are watching, Joan Penney, consider that even if you think this bread might be poison, the hogs are more deserving of fine gifts than you!"

My last pitch had so much fury and strength that the mud underneath my foot made me slip backward, and my head hit hard against the post.

"Ah, just like the rich father's prodigal son. Here she lies with the pigs after drinking too much ale," I heard as I regained consciousness. The cold rains on my face awakened me to see two men standing over me. With their mocking tones, the men chased the pigs away before the animals finished their feast.

"Mehitabel Downing, have you sunk so low to hide your drinking, so only the silent pigs will know? You foolish woman, look at what the hogs have done to your clothes. They might have eaten *you* up if we hadn't been nearby," said a man I knew for certain to be Job Smith.

"No, no, Goodman Smith." The taste of blood was upon my lips, and I reached to my head and felt the gash. "I had food in that basket, and the pigs must have eaten it," I replied, and then realized the foolishness of my claim. "I brought a gift of food to my mother, Joan Penney, to wish her well and—"

With scorn, the two men lifted me up before they retrieved my basket. They then saw the pigs had attempted to devour the basket along with the food, so they threw the basket back in the mud.

"Get on the cart, and we will take you to your husband. Such an unfortunate man. Surely, he regrets the day he married so foul and foolish a young girl. If his godly parents could see you now, they would be crying in heaven."

The ride of shame had again fallen upon me as it had when I accidentally set fire to Jacob Perkins' house. My explanations seemed so ridiculous, and the men did not believe my preposterous story.

My arrival was deeply upsetting to my young children. Sarah and Charles stood at the door of our home to witness their mother's shame. They both stepped back and held their hands over their mouths as I stumbled from the cart.

"John Downing, John Downing!" shouted the two men as they held me between them at our door. John was horrified at my disheveled appearance.

"Have you been in an accident, wife?" John opened the door wide and led me to the table near the hearth.

"John, your wife was found drunk and lying with the hogs. We came to help her out of the pen as the swine had torn at her clothes. Drunk, she was. Must have had quite a bit to drink and fell in with the hogs. That gash on her forehead will need care," Job Smith related. "Samuel Giddings here was with me. We both saw it."

Samuel turned to John and moved close to inform him further, "You know this must be reported to your tithingman. We are men of God who must lead those in perilous sin to turn from Satan to our almighty and forgiving God. Your wife has certainly tested God, hasn't she?" With those haunting words, both men left.

John and the children stood silently and stared and did not know what to do next.

"It wasn't as they say. I had no drink at all today. I know this to be true, but my head has a violent ache. I can remember little of what has happened." My head gyrated, and my body began to shake uncontrollably as I sat on the bench in my cold, drenched clothes. "I do not even know how I became as such, lying there with the swine. I lost awareness, and I don't remember how it happened. John, I can't defend myself. I feel ill ..." With my last words, I began to retch violently, and John scattered the children. Hannah tended to my wounds while I lay there as the room circled around me. I truly could not remember.

# CHAPTER THIRTY

As they promised, Samuel Giddings and Job Smith appeared before the Ipswich court on the 30th day of September in the year of our Lord 1684, to testify against me on the accusation of public drunkenness. The sound of the gavel had become too familiar, and its voice rang out that further indignity would be heaped upon me and those I loved.

Job Smith began, "Samuel and I stopped our work seeing storm clouds whipping up the wind and went to find shelter at the Cogswells' farm. Strikes of lightning were to the south, so we made our way to a small building where we heard the pigs' squeals. As we came closer, I saw a woman lying near the hogs, and two of the swine were tearing at her aprons and skirts. We shooed the hogs and dragged the woman out and saw it was Mehitabel Downing. We knew she was drunk and passed out. Her body must've been full of liquor, so she did not recognize the danger. We did what it teaches in the story of the Goodly Samaritan and took her home to her husband."

John Appleton was the chief magistrate of the court. As he listened, his head moved wearily from side to side. Their story melded with all the other tales he had ever heard about me. Appleton then asked Samuel Giddings if he had any testimony to add. Samuel just shook his head. "Your honor, what Job just said is all I know."

Appleton then turned to me, "Mehitabel Downing, will you plead guilty to this charge, or do you wish to bring testimony?"

"Sir, the events of this day could not have been as these men said. I had nothing to drink that morning before I went to the Penney farm. My servants can testify that I was on my way to see Goodwife Penney and to bring her jams and bread with only good intentions. I cannot remember how or why I was found with the swine."

I drew in a deep breath to dispel my weariness and summon up the courage to look straight at my accusers. "Indeed, Job and Samuel rescued me from the hogs, and for that I am grateful. That part is correct. I only know I suffered a great gash upon my forehead that remains, and I was wretchedly ill from the injury for many hours."

Those assembled on the benches behind me began to murmur and jeer. It had been sixteen years since I last stood before the magistrates accused of the crime of arson, but the people of Ipswich had long memories. Here I stood before the court as an adult woman, a mother, a wife, and a fully confessing member of the church. Any virtues I might have demonstrated since my marriage disappeared like a puff of smoke.

"It makes little sense, I am ashamed to say, but I am convinced the violent storms caused me to be in danger. I was not drunk, sir." There was nothing left for me to say.

Appleton noted the still visible wound upon my forehead, "The court agrees to consider your words although they ring hollow on their own. John Downing, what words do you have for the court on the matter of your wife and her accident?"

"Sir, I can only tell you of our servant, Hannah. She can give testimony to support what Mehitabel claims as true. I cannot testify about any facts from the morning of the visit, but I ask that Hannah give her testimony."

Hannah stood with a terrified look and approached the bench. This was her first time to give testimony in any court. She breathed in deeply to gain composure and then began, "I say Goodwife Downing worked with good intentions to prepare for her visit to her mother, Joan Penney, Richard Braybrooke's widow. John Downing has provided Goody Penney many services since the death of Richard Braybrooke, sirs. Mehitabel wished to make amends for any strife between them. I know this is true."

My eyes grew wide as I worried Hannah might go on with too many details, only to make my plight much worse. "Goody Downing spent two days preparing food to take to Joan and Thomas Penney. It was the best flour she used, and she added sweet molasses to the bread just as they do in Boston. It was a right fine gift. Mehitabel had only kind words to say as she left, and sir, I know she had no liquor in her. I know when she does and when she don't, I swear!" Hannah stepped back and put her hands over her lips. Revealing the truth of my fondness for drink could only work against me.

Appleton leaned forward and gave his proclamation. "Mehitabel Downing, we have two men who presented one story, but your loyal servant gives us another. We shall settle this at the next court meeting. Constable, you are to summon Thomas and Joan Penney to appear in court tomorrow morning. If what Hannah says is true, our witnesses can provide testimony. If not, Mehitabel, you will be sentenced at that time. Goody Downing, this is not your first time before the court, and any punishment will be more severe to bring you into correction." Appleton waved his hand at me in a dismissive manner and then continued, "Let the court move on to the next case of Richard Stackhous, ferryman of Salem, for not keeping his boat in good and safe condition for the country's service ..."

Job and Samuel's story portrayed me to be a woman far removed from God, and my just punishment from the Almighty was to be tormented by swine. Once again, my curse was magnified for all to witness. Once again, I brought shame to John, and now my children would be mocked and humiliated.

The words spoken in the past by Joan Penney rang in my ears. Her low opinion of me was vindicated, and I had to admit to myself that I had a fondness for drink. Ah, how it calmed my sorrow-filled heart!

Neither Joan nor Thomas Penney had reason to deliver testimony in my favor, yet at this time I had many questions of my own. Did I ever arrive at the entrance to their home? Was I perchance struck with lightning which caused my mind not to recall how I came to lie with the hogs? So typical of my life! I must struggle to remember, but it had been no use these days.

As we rode home, John held on tight to the reins, talking only to the horse, but expressed no anger toward me. He seemed pensive, not upset. He pulled back on the reins, bringing the cart to an abrupt stop and said, "We must turn around and visit with Reverend Hubbard and ask for his prayers. I have an unsettled feeling, and we should petition the Holy Ghost as our counselor. There is no hope if God is not with us tomorrow."

I put my arm through John's, hoping he would sense my gratitude. He turned the cart around and headed to the Hubbards' home. Sarah waited in the cart while John and I approached the entrance and knocked. A servant invited us into the foyer. "Please wait here while I fetch Mistress Hubbard."

Margaret Hubbard soon hobbled into the parlor, assisted by the servant and her walking stick. "John, Mehitabel, how good to see you both."

John bowed to our esteemed Mistress Hubbard. "We wish to speak with Reverend Hubbard about a serious matter."

Mistress Hubbard's countenance matched ours when she heard the request, "Oh, my husband had some business in Boston. I imagine he should arrive perhaps within hours or tomorrow or the next day at the latest. He has some additional business in Dedham. I am certain he will return with delightful news for us all."

John was desperate to let Mistress Hubbard know of the reason for our surprise visit. "Mistress Hubbard, we have need to pray. Mehitabel was summoned by the court because of an accident near the Penney farm and is accused of drunkenness. Our only witness is our servant who gave her testimony about the morning of the accident. She assured the court that Mehitabel was in good spirits and had no drink."

"John, what day is this of which you speak?" Mistress Hubbard replied.

"It was three days ago, Mistress, but Mehitabel received quite a blow to her head and remembers little. Mehitabel only knows she brought a gift of well-prepared food for Thomas and Joan in order to make amends. Our servant Hannah testified as such, but we fear Mehitabel was not believed. Now, Thomas and Joan are summoned to testify tomorrow morning. I can only imagine they will speak against her."

Mistress Hubbard became unsteady and fell into her chair. She raised her hands to embrace the frail layer of skin on her cheeks. It saddened me to see my news cause her distress, but then she surprised us with a renewed vigor.

"John, my husband came home three days ago after a visit to the Penneys' home and mentioned he had encountered Mehitabel on her foot journey to visit Joan. William found her in good spirits with gifts to bring to Thomas and Joan, as you say. He was especially heartened that Mehitabel had sincere forgiveness in her heart, but he had a fear that the outcome of Mehitabel's visit would not be a good one, and he asked Mehitabel to return home with him in his carriage. Mehitabel, you were not aware of what had just occurred at the Penney home. My husband's visit was not a pleasant one, but one to deliver correction. He had just chastised Joan Penney for her gossip and cold heart toward you."

It then became apparent I might have found the best witness to my real story: William Hubbard, the esteemed minister of Ipswich. While he might not arrive in time, his wife heard the story, and she could speak for me. My heart lifted when Margaret assured us she would be in court to give testimony about her husband's story. "I shall come even if my servants must carry my bed into the courtroom," Mistress Hubbard said with a determined smile.

Reverend Hubbard's story of delight in my good intentions might be my saving grace. I should have experienced a sleepless night, but the encouragement from Mistress Hubbard comforted me. As we rested that chilly October night, John held me in his arms. I believe he saw me in a different light now that my true story was unveiled. I knew I must prepare a clear testimony not tainted by all the confused and distorted events from that day.

# CHAPTER THIRTY-ONE

D read crept down my spine like a spider leaving its silky thread as John and I entered the meetinghouse. The ominous winds in this courtroom would confer either relief or a ruinous outcome. There sat Thomas and Joan Penney on the bench next to Job Smith and Samuel Giddings. Everyone was silent, their sour faces divulging that they were likely not pleased to miss such a fine day for harvesting their crops. Joan shook her head when she saw me enter and stared, her eyes like lightning on a pitch-black night.

John and I sat on a bench on the far side of the courtroom and held a place for Mistress Hubbard. Mr. Appleton pounded the rock upon the table to call the court to order. His first directive after prayer summoned Thomas and Joan Penney to come forward.

John leaped to his feet to alert the court of our notable witness. "Mr. Appleton, Mehitabel has a—"

Appleton slammed the rock on the table, "Goodman Downing, wait to speak until you are summoned!" He turned back to the Penneys. "Thomas Penney, did Mehitabel Downing come to your door on the 30th of September of this year to visit?"

Thomas spoke for both of them. "Yes, Mr. Appleton, Mehitabel Downing came uninvited and unwelcome, so I turned her away. She has brought nothing but sorrow to my poor wife, who has not been well. We want nothing to do with her, and I said as much."

John Appleton's eyebrows rose as he heard Thomas' bitter outburst. With his head crooked to the side, Mr. Appleton inquired, "And did Mehitabel Downing bring a gift of food for your wife?"

Joan glared at me as she stood by Thomas' side sharing in his brashness and arrogance. "I saw a basket and told her to go feed the hogs with it. We want nothing from the Downings."

At that moment, the meetinghouse door creaked open, and the courtroom burst into spontaneous murmurs. The bright sunlight illuminated the entrance as Mistress Hubbard stepped into the room with two servants at her side. The entire court was bewildered with the presence of Ipswich's most esteemed woman at these mundane court proceedings. Their whispers intensified when she made her way to the front of the meetinghouse.

"Mistress Hubbard, we are grateful but surprised by your presence. Do you wish to speak, or are you here as an observer?" Mr. Appleton inquired with great deference to our minister's wife. He signaled for the Penneys to be seated with a flippant wave of his hand.

Margaret Hubbard's gait was slow and halting, but there was an uncharacteristic boldness in her demeanor as she approached the bench. "Mr. Appleton, I come before you to give testimony on my husband's behalf. What I wish to say bears greatly on this case as I have heard it reported. May I speak to the court?"

"Most certainly, but please, you are invited to be seated and to speak from your bench," Mr. Appleton responded.

He rose from his lofty seat to escort Mistress Hubbard, who raised her hand to resist his gracious effort. "Sir, thank you, but I am in no need of special consideration."

With both servants to help steady the frail woman, she came closer to speak. "Sir, John and Mehitabel Downing came to my home yesterday to request prayers from their minister. My husband was away on church matters, and so they confided in me. The story of Mehitabel's summons was so distressing!"

Margaret Hubbard's voice remained calm as if the angels were guiding every word. "My good husband conveyed a relevant story to me upon his return from the Penneys' home. It was on the day of Mehitabel's visit. May I relate your minister's observations?"

With an affirmative sweep of his hand, Mr. Appleton granted permission for her testimony.

"Reverend Hubbard had left Thomas and Joan Penney after a visit to their home for church discipline when he observed Mehitabel Downing traveling by foot to visit the Penneys. He reported Mehitabel was of such a kind and contrite spirit on that day and had brought gifts of food for the Penneys. William mentioned one kind of bread most fashionable in Boston. I especially recall those words as I had no knowledge of the name of the bread, but I am most interested."

In the midst of her testimony, Mistress Hubbard peeked abruptly back at me. "Mehitabel, you must tell me how to make this bread. I do love fine bread." I smiled at her naivety and the sweetness of her words.

Mistress Hubbard returned my smile and continued her testimony. "Sirs, we have encouraged Mehitabel to offer forgiveness to her mother, although I consider the cruel treatment of Mehitabel by Goody Penney all these years to have been egregious. It is Joan Penney who should petition Mehitabel for forgiveness. I know I am a bold, old woman, but I have seen the actions of Joan Penney for many years. Both my husband and I have great sympathy for Mehitabel, this innocent child born out of her Father's sin."

A collective gasp came from those in attendance, and Joan's face lit up with rage. No one would dare utter words against those of our minister's saintly wife. That reality must have infuriated both Joan and Thomas.

"So, Mistress Hubbard," Mr. Appleton interjected, "your husband told you it was his impression that Mehitabel was going to the house of Joan and Thomas Penney with nothing but good intentions?"

"Yes, Mr. Appleton, my husband will have much to say about this matter to both you and the Penneys when he returns. I expect him tomorrow. He spoke nothing about any concern of excessive drinking but instead mentioned how well Mehitabel's face looked. Her health has been a concern to us since the death of her father, Richard. How Mehitabel ended up with the swine is a mystery, and it must have been a great tragedy that led her there."

Mistress Hubbard then turned to those who had given testimony against me. "Mehitabel had only good and kind intentions toward you, Goody Penney. You should be ashamed of how you treated Mehitabel, who only wanted to bring blessing into your life. And, Goodmen Smith and Giddings, I hope you now see that you have slandered Mehitabel! You incorrectly assumed she was drunk when you found her with the swine. With thunder and lightning brewing on that day, there could be any number of reasons for her accident."

Job Smith and Samuel Giddings lowered their heads and dared not make eye contact with the beloved minister's wife. Mistress Hubbard turned back to address the court in her usual soft manner. "Sirs, I apologize if my words are heated, but a great injustice has occurred. I would be a sinner and remiss if I did not defend the innocent."

All in the courtroom sat without a word whispered or mumbled. Mistress Hubbard's fiery testimony on my behalf displayed her righteous anger. This woman with a godly reputation had spoken, and no one dared to address the court after she walked up and embraced my hands.

Mister Appleton consulted the other magistrates and within a matter of minutes declared, "Mistress Hubbard, your words have given the court insight into how we shall proceed. Good woman, we hold your testimony in high esteem, and this case is dismissed. Mehitabel Downing, there are no witnesses who can testify as to what happened to cause you to fall within reach of the swine. We shall accept the testimony from Mistress Hubbard regarding your demeanor and good intentions as witnessed by our godly minister. All concerned may now leave the courtroom."

Although displays of affection are not proper in such a setting, I could not help but tenderly embrace the frail Mistress Hubbard and thank her for her assistance.

This esteemed old woman had grace and courage enough to make a bold endeavor to comfort me when I was beside myself with fear.

"John, you can do no greater service now than to truly love your wife. The Apostle Paul told us, '*Husbands, love your wives, even as Christ also loved the church, and gave himself for it*.' Go home and do as the Lord our God commands you," were the parting words of Mistress Hubbard.

And so we did, but a greater surprise than my vindication would be revealed upon Reverend Hubbard's return.

# Chapter Thirty-Two

The trees peeked above the corn's golden tassels as our horse trotted over the dusty roads on our journey home. Such an exquisite picture on this perfect day of my vindication! I breathed a deep sigh and put my hand into John's arm as the cart tussled us about. We did not speak, but Mistress Hubbard's words of wisdom sheltered John and me with a closeness we had not felt for months.

It was a blessing to be married to a patient man such as John. My transgressions and follies were at the root of all the problems that surfaced during our marriage, yet John never condemned me.

"John, I know my name will be forever linked to my past indiscretions and sins. That is a truth that cannot be denied. I am deeply sorry for the many burdens and improprieties I have brought to our marriage."

John's head nodded to accept my penitence. "Mistress Hubbard was correct to encourage us to walk in unity."

"John, we cannot continue to lead covert lives with one another. We must both be more open and honest to demonstrate our love and respect for each other."

John was a quiet and pensive man who preferred silence rather than to confront any problems set before him. It was a surprise when he began to address my concerns. "The inclinations that caused us to sin in the past are still part of our natures, Mehitabel, and the effects mold who we are. It is not natural for me to share what is deep in my heart."

We continued in silence and finally turned onto the path of our farm. John pulled back on the reins at the turn, and our cart came to a halt. He turned toward me and lovingly touched the wisps of hair peeking from my coif. His face was weary, but his eyes softened into a twinkle. "Mehitabel, you have grown wise with the years. My tendency is to bury my anguish and walk away. From this day forward, I resolve to consider you. That is the way God wants us to live as man and wife, but know this: my love for you has never faltered. You must rest assured."

John's few but loving words were a struggle for him to convey, but I knew that he always intended only good toward me. How blessed I was to be the wife of such a humble and honorable man!

The thought of Joan then came to my mind, and I pitied her in a marriage to such a contemptible man. Unfortunately, she would always be part of my life, but it would be prudent not to have her as my sworn enemy. My summons to the court showed there was no gift I could bestow upon Joan that would ever change her opinion of me.

Late next evening, well after sunset, I heard a knock at the door and opened it with caution. Colin, one of the Hubbards' most trusted servants, stood before me. "Goody Downing, I beg your forgiveness for this late visit, but Reverend and Mistress Hubbard ask that you come to their home tomorrow morning. They add the matter is of great importance."

"Are they well? Is there a concern of which I should be aware?"

"I am not privy to the details of their request, but can assure you all is well," replied Colin. "They have one more message. Your visit will require the entire day."

With the Hubbards' strange request delivered in such a pleasant manner, Colin went back out into the darkness of night.

Always predisposed to despair, I pondered if Reverend Hubbard's words to his wife were misrepresented in court. Might it be my plight that the accusations had not truly ended? Reverend Hubbard would surely have requested me to come immediately if there was any bad news. Perhaps he had summoned Mr. Appleton to retract his wife's words of testimony. What could be of such great importance that I would be required to set aside a great deal of my day? Would I be brought into correction by the courts once again?

My worries needed to be laid to rest, and so I began to make preparations for tomorrow's adventure. Perhaps it was best to bring some molasses bread as a courtesy to Mistress Hubbard's courtroom request. Hannah taught me to combine equal parts of the finest cornmeal, rye, and wheat flours and lay the bread upon oak leaves as it steamed. I proceeded to make the Boston-style bread with my own hands so that it would be a true gift.

As I left the next morning, I told John of the request from the Hubbards but did not reveal the speculations that belied my fears. When I reached the bottom of the Hubbards' steps, my heart whispered a prayer that all would go well and the scores of adverse possibilities would not occur.

The knocker's loud clank announced my arrival, and Colin greeted me with a polite comment about the agreeable weather. He escorted me into the Hubbards' comfortable parlor and asked me to sit in their finest, embroidered chair. My limbs quivered as I waited in anticipation. I leaped to my feet when Mistress Hubbard entered the parlor on the arm of her husband.

Reverend Hubbard's broad smile relieved some of my anxiety, and then he spoke with great deference. "Mehitabel, we thank you for your promptness and hope the day will allow you to spend many hours with us. We all have a journey ahead, but we should inform you of this mysterious adventure. Please sit."

"Mistress Hubbard, I brought these loaves of the Boston Brown Bread made with molasses, rye, and cornmeal. It is what you asked about in the courtroom," I said while presenting my modest gift.

"Then we shall enjoy some now to give us strength for our journey. We shall save one of these loaves for ..." Mistress Hubbard hesitated with a mischievous smile, "for our trip."

Reverend Hubbard sat at the edge of his seat. "Mehitabel, I believe God spoke to my heart after we met upon the road last week when I saw you carrying that basket with gifts for the Penneys. I sensed the time might be right for me to try to find your real mother's whereabouts, although I was concerned she might have perished. While on church business with my associates in Boston, I inquired about her. One of them, Reverend John Danforth, the minister from Dorchester, knew of a woman by that name. He told me she had remarried and now lived in Dedham. Your mother, at the time of your birth, was Alice Elyss."

My heart fluttered with joy as I recalled Alice's face and sweet disposition. My hope was that Reverend Hubbard would continue with a tale of good news.

"After my business with my colleagues concluded, I traveled to the parish in Dedham to see if Alice was still living." Reverend Hubbard hesitated and after a long pause exclaimed, "I found her! Mehitabel, I found her to be a widow and living as a servant.

"I persuaded her master that Alice should come with me. We arrived late last evening, and I took her to the ordinary nearest to our home. I did not want the excitement and commotion to concern my wife, who I feared might not be well. I assure you; Margaret promptly scolded me for not inviting Alice to be our guest. Obadiah Woods and his wife promised a suitable room at the tavern."

"My mother, Alice—the one I met while in prison—is at the ordinary? Are you telling me I will meet her today?" Tears of joy streamed down my face. My deepest wish was about to come true.

Reverend Hubbard's visage radiated delight as he observed my joyful response. Apparently, he fully understood the impact his discovery had made. He kneeled before my chair and gathered my hands in his. Our good minister had always been kind to me, even in his delivery of discipline, but this was the first time he had ever touched me. I leaned forward and impulsively kissed his cheek. My spontaneous boldness was received by Reverend Hubbard not with disapproval but with an even wider smile.

My mind was like a whirlwind as we traveled to the tavern. My heart beat intensely, and a perpetual smile was upon my face as I listened to the details of how Alice was found. We arrived at the tavern, and Obadiah's wife, Hazelelponah, came hustling in our direction when she saw me, signaling us with her hand. "Mehitabel, come this way. Your mother and I have been chatting so much, so she took it upon herself to come to the kitchen to keep me company with my chores. Such a godly woman is your mother! If she lived here in Ipswich, we would be good friends; I know it." Hazelelponah led me to a table and brought us a large bowl of rabbit stew. "She made this stew just this morning. I will fetch Alice. Eat!"

The Hubbards and I had just tasted our first bite when Alice appeared at the kitchen entrance. Reverend Hubbard stood to greet her again, "Greetings to you, good woman. You should know my wife scolded me that I did not invite you to spend the night as our guest, but now I can see you have been well taken care of by Hazelelponah."

Alice stood frozen. Overwhelmed with emotion, she clasped her hands to her chest and appeared not to know what she should do next. I came quickly to her side and put my arms around her, resting my head against her chest for just a moment. Alice stroked my head and then tightened our embrace. My years of longing culminated in this moment, and now all was right with the world.

"Mother, I am so sorry I did not know it was you who came to visit me in prison. I can now see myself and my daughter Sarah as I look at your face and your hair." I wanted to say so much more but was overtaken by a sea of happiness and gratitude. I had finally met my mother.

There was so much I wanted her to know. I wished to tell her about John, her four beautiful grandchildren, and my home. I didn't want her to know of my many failures or to learn that many in town had been so cruel to me.

Mistress Hubbard embraced her old friend, Alice. "A tavern is not the place for you and Mehitabel to discuss such intimate things. My husband and I will move this blessed reunion to our home." She turned to Hazelelponah. "Thank you and to your husband for your gracious hospitality."

"Yes, but I also wish for John and the children to meet you, Alice." To call her Alice did not seem right, yet the name of "Mother" left me with bitter memories of Joan.

"What shall I call you? The name of Alice for my mother does not seem right."

"Oh, I hadn't thought about that. I was born in Wales and was just a young girl when my parents came to the colony. In Wales, we called our mothers 'Mam.' Does Mam sound like what you would like to call me?"

*Mam.* The name sounded like what a young child would say when they asked something of their dear mother. Mam.

"Mam is an excellent name for you, and I shall instruct the children that you are to be known as Grandmam Alice. How does that title sound to you?"

We all laughed at the charm of the name. Mam sat next to me in the back of the carriage and told me about her childhood in Wales as we rode to the Hubbards' home. Her stories filled the hole in my heart just as I dreamed they would.

# CHAPTER THIRTY-THREE

A flock of geese descended from the air into the fields as Alice and I walked on the soft grasses. Their gentle plummet from the heavens reminded me that Alice was the dearest gift I could have hoped for. We were eager to spend the little time given to us. She told me of her four children, all in different towns, and her husband, Gregory, ten years now gone. The stories of her parents' struggles during their early years in the colonies taught me of the plight of those who arrived already as servants. In desperation, her parents were forced to indenture the entire family throughout the nearby villages. Mam entered into service at the Braybrooke home in 1651.

We became intimately acquainted during the three days she spent with John and me. Alice's visit made it seem as if she had always been a loyal friend. She knew about me while I was in the depths of despair, and the secrets of our souls now seemed natural to share.

"How did your husband, Gregory, treat you because of your child born out of wedlock? Did your other children know about my birth?" The questions might have seemed intrusive, but Mam answered them nonetheless.

"Mehitabel, Gregory knew of my sin, but he also understood the circumstances of a master and a young serving girl. He himself was indentured for seven years. I was a lovely girl in my youth." Mam hesitated as she knew that to discuss such private matters was improper. "You are a married woman with children. You understand. I do not want to speak against the memory of your dear father or place blame on your stepmother. She was the one who bore the stripes of a whip not upon her back but upon her heart." Alice looked down and began to weep. The bitter memory of her sin disclosed that she realized how her deed had affected Joan.

Those sweet moments with Mam reminded me of how I was denied a mother's tender words and affection during my childhood.

"Mam, I have been abundantly loved by Father, my husband, my children, and Mistress Hubbard. Reverend Hubbard has shown me kindness and God's mercy and correction. But Joan was not as a mother should have been. I tried to understand her hurts, but her treatment of me as her stepdaughter was far worse than one treats a servant or a slave. A servant knows she has no right to be treated kindly by her master, but a child should be confident of a mother's constant and genuine love."

Mam softly embraced me, then released me to stand face to face. She caressed my hands in hers. "Mehitabel, from afar I have known of your journey. I see in you a woman who struggles to be strong, to be a good wife and daughter. I see a woman who has quarried deep inside to overcome the challenges God has allowed in your life."

Our discourse halted when we heard the echoes of a garrison of men marching to the nearby training field. Mam pointed to the fine regiment. "Child, look how those men dress. They arose this morning and made proper decisions on what should be worn and chose each part of their uniform with care. You must do the same, although you must instead wrestle against the principalities and powers of darkness. Mehitabel, you have been fighting against your flesh, but the wiles and wickedness of the Devil have at times defeated you. Look at those men carefully."

Each man was outfitted differently, but they all had the same defensive weapons.

"Dear, you must gird your waist with the truth—the truth that you are a child of God, one of his elect, and nothing could be more precious. The breastplate like the soldiers wear is to protect your heart. Know you are as one righteous with God. The shields they use are to safeguard us from the fiery darts that the wicked one rains down upon our heads and hearts. The soldiers' swords and knives are most important, as they help take back the ground the enemy has stolen. Our sword is the very Word of God. Only then, Mehitabel, is a soldier ready for battle! You must stand your ground, and don't let the Evil One and his minions, who sometimes come to us in human form, take what God has given you as his adopted child."

Words about war and fighting seemed suitable for a man who must protect his family and his town. Never had I regarded these images as appropriate for a woman. The task of a wife and mother was not to fight, but Mam advised that I must use the resources God had given me to battle Satan. These words of Scripture I had heard so often now came alive for me.

"Mehitabel, I am concerned it is not just you who needs to heed these words. I fear many in the colony walk in the clouds and cannot see their way. Such is the darkness of these days with neighbor accusing neighbor of great wickedness and allegiance to Satan."

"Reverend Hubbard warns us of such evils, Mam. I shall be on guard against the Evil One."

From a distance, we saw the figure of a person emerge from the softly rounded hills. As we neared, I recognized it was a woman I both pitied and dreaded. "Oh, that woman you see at a distance is Rachel Clinton. She has had a most miserable life, and I am grateful I have not been burdened as she."

Mam replied, "I recall long ago her father had great wealth, but her mother's troubled mind caused much despair in their lives. Rachel will be commended by our good God for being the only child to care for her mother. I believe her mother was declared insane."

"Yes, Father gave witness in court that Rachel's relatives had treated her poorly. They denied her any rights to her parents' estate. She also married poorly—a man named Lawrence, much younger than she. Charged with abandonment and had several children out of wedlock while still married to Rachel. She sought a divorce, but life and the courts have only handed her disappointments. She is forced to beg in town."

My voice trailed off as Rachel approached us. Father always instructed me to treat her with kindness, so I greeted her with cheer. "Rachel, how goes it with you today? Is not the sun's warmth in October a gracious gift?"

"Goody Downing. I have not seen you for many days. Is this a guest you have in your house?" Rachel inquired.

"Yes, Rachel. This is Alice from Dedham. Please go to our home and tell Sarah she is to give you a portion of our midday meal. Mam ... I mean Alice, made some corn porridge with ham." I was flustered as I had revealed too much. Rachel could not be trusted even on a good day.

"Goody Downing, I would be most grateful for my belly to be full today. Goodman Boreman has told horrible stories about me all throughout the village. Many in town turn to hide when they see me on the road."

As we walked, Rachel peered closely at Alice to study her face. "Did we not know each other many years ago, Goody? You are the Alice who left Ipswich more than a score of years ago after you were whipped for fornication, are you not?"

Alice drew in a quiet breath, clearly not certain of how she should react. "Yes, I was but a young girl as were you, in those early years in Ipswich."

Rachel sneered at Alice with contempt and snorted loudly. "My husband—he is still my husband—has a whore who was our serving girl. An indentured contract she had! They have three bastard children, and still, the courts will not grant me a divorce. Fornicating with a master has given both you and Lawrence's whore a life better than my own!"

I could not bear to hear Mam insulted by such a deranged woman, yet I knew Satan's hold had broken Rachel's spirit, and she was to be pitied. "Rachel, please go ahead and ask Hannah for some food. We wish you well."

As Rachel continued on the path to our home, she muttered, "Hellhound ... serving girl!" in a tone of disgust.

I wrapped my arms around Mam and led her to a nearby roughly hewn bench. Mam sighed and looked away in embarrassment. "Mehitabel, our days together are near their end, and I am sorry we had to witness Rachel's scourge. Her malicious words are what a sinner such as I must endure. Our transgressions are often not forgotten by others."

It grieved my heart to know Alice would soon depart and before long would be but a beautiful memory. Our time together should not be marred by the trials of others. I wanted only to gather up her words and affections like a bouquet of yellow and gold flowers. They would shelter me from the storms that would surely blow into my life in the years to come.

## CHAPTER THIRTY-FOUR

## WINTER, 1692

"John, I am so weary of this winter. This snow has been pummeling us for days at a time, with no respite in sight." I gazed at the steady stream of snowflakes from our bedroom window. John secured the warming pan at the foot of our bed, and we nestled under the covers.

"Digging a path to the barn is my primary chore as of late. Just like caring for the animals—never ending," said John before he drifted off in his well-earned slumber.

John and I were both asleep when a pounding on the door shook our bed. In my night fog, I thought it was snow thunder, but then the very room began to shake from the blows to the door. John raced down the stairs to secure his gun. The pounding continued but was muffled by the plea, "John Downing, open the door!"

"Who goes there? Give me your name!" yelled John.

"Elias, Elias Trask."

"John lifted the bar from the hatch and hurried in his old friend. "Elias, what brings you out in this weather?"

Elias stomped his boots and shook the snow off his hat. "John, I came to warn the neighbors. We all need to be on alert! There was an attack today in York on the settlement along the river. Hundreds of English have been injured, scores killed, and near the whole village burnt to the ground."

John shuttled Elias to the hearth, and I placed a blanket over his shoulders and offered him a warm cup of rum.

"The first shots were sounded near Moulton's Tavern. The Abenaki tribe lay in wait and systematically broke into every home and slaughtered the English."

"You say many have been killed, but still some survived?" asked John.

"Many barricaded themselves in the garrison house. I heard the stories straight from those terrorized people who found refuge in Salem. They told of the most profane killings. Reverend Hubbard's close associate in York was readying to visit a sick congregant, and the savages shot him while he was still upon his horse. They left his body naked and tortured. Reverend Dummer's wife and young son were taken captive."

Our children and servants who had joined us stood frozen after hearing the news. Elias rose from his seat and said, "I came only to give warning. You and your sons keep those muskets handy, and take care any time you leave this house."

"We leave the safety of our homes only to feed the animals each day and our souls on Sunday," I said.

"Ipswich has been spared from the worse so far, so I can only advise you to stay alert. I have but one more stop before I can rest my bones. God's blessing and protection upon you." Elias slipped out into the bitter winds and mounted his horse to journey to the next house.

Gray thoughts colored our minds with despair in the following weeks. Our isolation from the Motherland compounded the anxious mood in the colony, as we had no ready army to call upon for our protection.

The cold and snow continued. In early February, news of strange happenings in nearby Salem Village added to our thoughts that Satan had indeed unleashed his minions in our neighboring villages. The supernatural was part of everyday life in Puritan New England, and there was a pervasive belief that Satan was present and active on earth. Give the Devil any opportunity, and he would snatch you up. All the misfortunes of life could be blamed on the work of the Devil.

The hysteria in Salem Village began after Doctor Griggs was summoned to examine the sudden mysterious behaviors of Reverend Parris' six-year-old daughter, Betty, and twelve-year-old niece, Abigail. The doctor's only explanation for their fits, screams, and writhing was that the evil hand of witchcraft was upon them. The belief that witches targeted children made the doctor's diagnosis seem increasingly likely.

Soon, these two young girls accused Reverend Parris' Indian slave, Tituba, and two ne'er-do-well women in Salem Village of practicing witchcraft on them. Then a frenzy of other accusations exploded amongst the villagers and was allowed to run free. The charge of witchcraft was so convenient, and sound reasoning played no part in some people's explanations. Mary Edwards claimed Rachel Clinton cast a spell on her pigs and five of them died. Accusations such as this made complete sense to many people.

Perceived injustices from long ago were now remembered and paired with new hostility. Long ago, Ann Putnam Sr. alleged that Rebecca Nurse had inflicted her with a curse, causing her to miscarry several children. Ann now accused Rebecca of appearing to her at night in her white shift and nightcap, threatening to tear Ann's soul out of her body if she would not sign the Devil's red book.

The friends of these afflicted girls soon joined in with stories about the invisible spirits of witches pinching, choking, and biting the innocent. Tales of secret gatherings in the forest openings and visions of demonic yellow birds nursing from a mole between a witch's fingers were told over and over again.

Villagers conjured up new explanations of past afflictions, always with the Devil and his earthly toadies in mind. George Burroughs, the former minister of Salem village, was driven out ten years ago by those in alliance with the Putnams. Burroughs was brought from Maine to face charges of being a dreadful wizard who had supernatural strength and powers. He stood before the Court of Oyer and Terminer in Salem, accused of "bewitching his first two wives to death." The accusing girls had visions of his deceased wives telling them of their murders.

When the dreary snows lifted, we all hoped and prayed for a renewal of our spirits, but it was not to be. The seeds of suspicion had already been deeply planted along with the grains and kernels in the muddy fields. Tales of sundry acts of witchcraft, spun alongside the spinning of the sheep's wool, encouraged new accusations each day. Satan's forces recruited weak-minded townspeople to join with their mighty demonic army and trample upon us. It was now safer to be afflicted than accused, and so the accusations spiraled out of control.

Hardy tufts of grass peeked out from the snow on the winding road. The horses' hoof prints disappeared in the dwindling slush as John and I journeyed to the Proctor Tavern to discuss a land lease with John Proctor. Proctor rented land and the tavern on the estate where my husband grew up—the lands of Emanuel Downing.

"Visiting my father's old tavern brings back memories," John said. "Do you know that when I was just seven, I tapped into a new keg of Father's best rum in the storage room, courtesy of my brother James? My mother was livid when she discovered me in a stupor. Banned James from the main house for a month, she did."

Proctor's three brown and white hounds yipped and howled as we approached the tavern. They wagged their tails in a friendly greeting while John assisted me from the carriage. From the corner of my eye, I detected the flash of a young woman's figure bolting from the side door. She ran past us, pulling her apron over her face, but not before we recognized her. There was something unsettling about Mary Warren; most people thought her problems stemmed from when she lived through the violent Indian attacks that killed her entire family. She came to Ipswich as an orphan and had few friends because of her skittish disposition.

Although near twenty, she was more like a wayward, disheveled child than a godly young woman.

John shook his head at the sight of Mary, and we proceeded to the entrance. The tavern had taken on a quiet, sullen tone these days as townspeople now greeted one another in a guarded fashion, their eyes darting back and forth as they inspected people who passed. They hunched together in small groups, looking over their shoulders or peering around a corner, and as new people entered the tavern, they would turn their heads away and whisper so their gossip could not be overheard. No one wanted their conversations carried to the courts. Often, a person entering the door triggered a connection to the newest accusations or misgivings, and the chatter resumed. Taverns everywhere became fertile breeding grounds for suspicions and worries.

Proctor approached us with a warm embrace, but the surrounding murmurings told us all was not well. He led us to a table far away from other ears and shook his head. "John, Mehitabel, I am confounded by the wickedness of some of our young people and even more confounded by their elders who must be in league with the Devil."

My gaze flitted around the room to survey who might overhear our words. "Goodman Proctor, are you speaking of those girls in Salem Village? With their fits and quick tongues in the courtroom, they speak death to those they accuse."

Proctor nodded. "To accuse Parris' Indian slave Tituba and impoverished women such as Sarah Good and Sarah Osborne can be understood. But now the Putnams' daughter accuses Martha Corey's specter of inflicting her. Says the specter pinched and choked her during the night. It is her mother, Ann Putnam Sr., who has put her daughter up to this treachery! Sarah Good's daughter Dorothy is also under suspicion of cavorting with the Devil. How can a four-year-old child stand accused? The moral and wise are in chains under these claims of witchcraft and its darkness."

John rested his elbow on the table and leaned forward, "Proctor, who can stand up to Satan and to these girls in Salem Village? The righteous perish with the wicked. We ourselves speak to hardly a soul for fear we might be falsely accused."

Proctor looked around with trepidation. "True, most are afraid. No one but I have declared that the Reverend Samuel Parris is unworthy to be called a man of God. Parris' perverse daughter and niece were the first accusers, yet they are regarded as innocents. More foolish girls have come forward to add to the accusations of innocent townsfolk. The villagers are so gullible; they insist that these children could never be in allegiance with the Devil."

John nodded in agreement. "God's Holy Word tells us that a minister must manage his own household well with dignity and keep his children submissive. If the reverend doesn't know how to manage his own family, how will he care for God's people?"

I shook my head, giving credence to John's words. "We only need to remember when I was a youth. The young are not always innocent. Oh, how I ask God's forgiveness each time I think of my foolishness at Jacob Perkins' house. I understand how a child's heart thinks and feels. We saw Mary Warren as she left the tavern just now, and my heart aches for her and the others she is aligned with."

"Aye, you saw Mary Warren leaving? Let me tell you why she stormed out of the tavern." Proctor moved in even closer. "Mary began having fits soon after the strange happenings at Samuel Parris' house a few weeks back. I tell you, these girls all lie and pretend they are bewitched. Mary's fits and contortions in court stopped after I gave her a good beating. Kept her at the spinning wheel, and her fits never returned. The Devil knows that idleness best serves his desires. I told her just now that perhaps she deserves another beating. Lazy, worthless serving girl."

"Goodman Proctor, John and I caution you to be more prudent. It is likely Mary will run back to that gaggle of foolish girls and speak falsely against you. Those wicked girls will accuse you as they have done others, and you would surely be brought to court to face their lies. Promise you will be less harsh with Mary, for your sake," I pleaded, "and for Elizabeth's."

"Mehitabel, I thank you for your concern. I remember long ago when your father and I disagreed. Do you remember how Richard brought me into accountability? He and I became steadfast friends for the rest of his days." Proctor's face lightened with the fond recollection. "Your father never hesitated to stand up to townspeople for their mistreatment of others. I still recall how he spoke to the town magistrates for Rachel Clinton about the abuse she suffered at the selfish acts of her family. She would have been destitute if not for the courage of your father. I resolve to speak the truth as I see it, just as Richard did. God wants us to speak against the sins of others, for surely the Devil is prowling in Ipswich and Salem and will devour us if we do not stand against him!"

Proctor's kind words about my father warmed my heart, but he needed to calm his temperament. My husband leaned back against the wall and sighed. "John Proctor, I fear you speak the truth. God is a great deal angrier with those deceivers in our congregation than He is with the sinners who are now in the flames of hell."

Encouraged by my husband's bold words, John Proctor spoke in a voice that could be heard throughout the tavern. "The wrath of God burns against them, and their damnation will not slumber. The pit and fires are prepared; the furnace is now scorching and ready to receive them. The flames now rage and glow!"

All eyes and ears were upon John Proctor. He pounded on the table and a bulging vein pulsed in his forehead. "I tell you both the truth in this matter. I would rather have paid forty pounds than have Mary Warren align with those girls during their accusations. This madness would stop if these girls were all whipped at the post. I had to fetch that jade, Mary Warren, just this morning after Rebecca Nurse's examination. I should not have let her spend the night in Salem Village. If those girls were left to speak as they wished, we would all be named witches and devils. I say this madness would stop if they were kept away from each other!"

I needed to pray God's protection on John Proctor and his tongue. John and I had learned over these past years that our words might come back to haunt us. A bravery of spirit such as Proctor's was rare, but these days it was a foolish virtue.

As we rode home, John and I discussed the situation. We knew Proctor was right. We also knew he would pay a heavy price if some in Salem were made aware of his thoughts. A righteous person would suffer for being on the side of sensibility and truth. What we did not know was that another curse was about to fall upon me, and that scourge would be the most unjust of all.

# CHAPTER THIRTY-FIVE

The spring of 1692 ushered in more accusations against innocent townspeople in the colony. Some said it was because of the divide in Salem Village's congregation: those who supported Reverend Parris and those who thought him haughty and inept. Even more devious were a few like Ann and Thomas Putnam, Parris supporters, who bore the sin of envy against their more prosperous neighbors.

These terrible embers of lies erupted into a mighty dragon, fed more by new names and more heinous stories of the Devil's work. Ann Foster, herself amongst the accused, blamed Martha Corey for the appearance of the Devil in the form of an exotic bird who promised her prosperity and the gift of afflicting at a glance. Stories of sorcery with poppets, a Devil's Sabbath in the meadow, and bewitched dogs both terrified and fascinated the villagers.

The hideous rains of evil poured on both the righteous and the unrighteous. Samuel Endicott accused Mary Bradbury, a gospel woman, of assuming the form of a blue boar and others said she sold bewitched butter to a sea captain causing violent storms at sea. Satan's delusions closed almost every heart and threw a thick veil over wisdom and understanding.

In early April, Mary Warren tacked a note on the door of the meetinghouse requesting prayers of thanks for her release from Satan's spell. All who read the message hoped the Devil's minions had finally disappeared from the colony. When asked to explain the note, Mary's only response was: "The afflicted persons did but dissemble." Not understanding her words, the congregation questioned her further and inferred Mary meant the accusing girls were lying. Unfortunately, Mary quickly disclaimed this line of reasoning, and the diabolical molestations and accusations resumed.

John Proctor concluded that Mary Warren had learned the error of her evil ways and thought it safe to leave Ipswich on business for a few days. As soon as he left, Mary joined the girls in court, this time as a witness. Mary now accused Elizabeth Proctor, John's wife, of witchcraft. Our hopes of peace were dashed.

It wasn't long before my husband brought more dreaded news from a meeting at the ordinary. Proctor's brazen comments had come back to harm him with a vengeance. During her testimony against Goody Proctor, Mary Warren also accused John Proctor of being a warlock.

A pained and weary gaze rested on my husband's face. "Mehitabel, we have much to fear now that Proctor has been accused." He shook his head in disbelief and sat at the table, stroking his chin. "I now agree with the sentiments of the Quakers. They believe God intends to punish Puritans for hostility toward their sect. Surely we have done the Quakers a great injustice with the beatings."

I covered my mouth and breathed deeply through my fingers. "This is as we feared for Goodman Proctor since Mary Warren accused his wife of witchcraft last week. Prison will be a most fearsome place for a woman with child. Mary Warren has done the Proctors much damage."

John looked about the house to make sure no servants could overhear our discussion. "Yes, the villagers who witnessed the testimony report that those girls and Mary Warren testified to the most horrible tortures and convinced the jurors with their writhing and frenzy. Mary testified that Proctor's specter beat her, and the Devil himself tried to force her to write in his book."

My voice lowered to a whisper. "Our words of testimony could be easily misunderstood to accuse us rather than provide support to those who are innocent. Remember how Samuel Sibley repeated stories about Proctor? We both were there at the tavern when Proctor boasted of his threats against the accusers and how he had beaten Mary Warren."

"Sibley repeated Proctor's words to the court. Mehitabel, we cannot suffer the same fate as the Proctors. Signing any petition of support would be grounds to force us to testify. Those scurrilous words John Proctor spoke to us last month at the tavern have come back to haunt us all. We must trust no one."

To sign a petition of support for Elizabeth and John Proctor would surely result in our being amongst the accused. My husband and I resolved to remain silent with only prayers given up for our friends.

This whirlwind of deception had fallen upon our towns, but I wanted to do something to help the innocent now sitting in prison for months. Fear now froze any thoughts, or they spun frantically in my mind. A pungent melancholy dwelt in my soul as memories of my youth flooded back. I understood how an innocent and confused person could react as they stood before the officials in court. I remembered the jeers and mocking words from the townspeople. I knew the wretchedness of weeks of imprisonment with criminals—the guilty, the insane, and the destitute. I prayed to God to help me know what to do.

Reverend William Hubbard was cautious during these times, for he knew Satan had a stranglehold on both the foolish and the devious. His sermons overflowed with words of vigilance. He cautioned us not to allow our minds to be carried off into the darkness. In late May, Pastor Hubbard spoke with great urgency about our duty to testify to the truth. To lie about Satan was an affront to God, he said, and someday our Lord and Creator would hold us under His severe judgment.

After the accusations against the Proctors, the Sunday meeting overflowed with scores of despairing villagers. Across the room, Mary Warren sat alone, tapping her heels and rocking and rocking. She turned around and glared at the faces of the congregants but abruptly turned away when they returned her stare.

Mary ambled out of the meetinghouse, appearing to talk to herself and shaking her head in anguish. Was she overwhelmed with guilty thoughts of her wicked accusations about the Proctors? My motherly spirit welled up inside of me. Her own mother had died at the hands of the savages not that long ago, and my daughter Sarah was close in age to Mary. I prayed God might give me the conviction to speak to her.

The accusing girls now shunned Mary, so she walked alone on the dusty path. The town did not know if Mary was truly one of the afflicted or had gone to Satan's side. I readied my step until I came alongside her and then took a deep breath. "Good day, Mary. Do you know who I am?"

She stared at me suspiciously and nodded, "You are Goody Darling, John Darling's wife. I have seen you about the village."

"Yes, I am John's wife, but my name is Mehitabel Downing, not Darling."

Mary's cheeks flushed, and a tentative smile came across her face. She seemed pleased a respectable person would talk with her.

"Mary, I believe I understand your struggles. I was somewhat similar to you during my youth. I was blessed to have Mistress Hubbard befriend me, and I would do the same for you if you like."

She stared at me with no reply. I closed my eyes for just a moment, and then took a calming breath. "Mary, our God is an all-knowing God. He understands our hearts as well as our minds. Please consider that you can stop—simply stop—any accusations that may not be true. These other girls have frightened you more than your fear of the wrath of God. John and Elizabeth Proctor are bold and spirited people but surely not as you and the girls say. I have always known them as good and honest church members."

Suddenly, a crazed look transformed Mary's blank face. "Are you a servant in their home? You know nothing of Satan's work in their house. They are spiteful and wicked and unjust and deserve God's wrath, for their wickedness could only have come from the Devil!"

The repulsive stare in Mary Warren's eyes told me that my encounter with her had been a grave mistake. I knew our meeting should end, but my heart did not listen to my mind.

I put my hand on her arm and looked into her eyes, "Mary Warren, it is not as you say. None of this can be. There is another judgment, dear child. To lie or deceive before God is an even more serious matter than to lie before the courts."

Mary's voice rose. "You, Goody Darling, should be more careful than to befriend those who seek others to sign the book of the Devil. You know not what I have seen and suffered. Have the Proctors asked you also to sign the Devil's book?"

I backed away as she turned abruptly and left. I grasped my trembling hands and tried to focus my thoughts so that fear would not overtake my entire body. I intended good but had instead created a foul enemy.

# CHAPTER THIRTY-SIX

I constantly fretted during the days that followed my encounter with Mary Warren. My heart pounded wildly even when I was at rest and seemed to leap from my chest when the door opened. My intention was only to help her, but my name could be cast upon the heap of the accused.

The following Saturday, John walked through the door, his eyes full of both weariness and sadness. He threw his hat on the table and asked me to sit next to him at the hearth. "Mehitabel, I have just received notice from Mr. Denison. An accusation has been made against you ..." he sighed deeply, "by Mary Warren."

My heart was prepared for this possibility. "John, I knew that my encounter with Mary Warren was ill-fated. Please forgive me." John reached out and took both of my hands in his as I continued, "The women suspected of witchcraft in Ipswich and Gloucester have all been godly church members. If such godly and prominent women as Margaret Prince, Phoebe Day, and Elizabeth Dice were charged, how could I expect not to be included?"

"Mehitabel, we shall pray now and try not to consider the worst. The children and I will be at your side and will pray for God to protect you from the wickedness of these times." John held me close, and we sobbed. We prayed throughout the night for God to lift this ordeal and to protect our daughter Sarah's engagement to Thomas Lufkin.

When we arrived at court the next morning, I was shocked to see Rebecca Nurse and Elizabeth Proctor seated on the bench reserved for the accused. Behind them was George Burroughs, a former Salem Village pastor. I started to wonder if John had misunderstood. Maybe I was only here as a witness. It soon became apparent from the downcast eyes all around me that my fate was the same as these godly people who sat before the court.

The Court of Judicature was called to order, and the magistrate proceeded to call the four of us forward. I continued to be confused until I heard our names read in the summons:

"Mr. George Burroughs, Rebecca Nurse, Elizabeth Proctor, Mehitabel Downing, you have been brought before this court to hear the testimony given this first day of June, in the year of our Lord, 1692. Mary Warren has given testimony that a fortnight ago, the specters of Mr. George Burroughs, Goody Nurse, Goody Proctor, and Goody Downing had come upon her whilst in prison in Salem and did cause great terrors. They tried to make her sign a paper to the Devil with a red mark."

Goody Nurse looked down, shaking her head. Reverend George Burroughs sat rigidly on the bench, his arms across his chest. Elizabeth Proctor rocked back and forth as if she wanted to comfort the innocent babe in her womb. All three of those accused with me had been summoned from their prison cells many times to face their accusers and the court. How easily an innocent could be swept into this mire! I would not suffer their fate; I would fight against this injustice!

The magistrate signaled for me to approach the bench. I breathed deeply to gain composure then moved forward. But instead of allowing me to begin my testimony, the judge asked only how I wished to plead: guilty or innocent.

"I am truly innocent and have never conspired with Satan. Mary Warren accuses me falsely. I warned her before her imprisonment that to lie before God was more egregious than lying to this court!"

"It was surely you, Goody Darling!" Mary Warren shouted from the other side of the judge's bench. "I saw you as clearly as the others, and you held the book of the Devil. You did!" Her eyes glared with wickedness from Satan himself.

"Your Honors, Mary Warren mistakes me for Goody Darling. Mary Warren called me by the name Goody Darling many times when she talked to me that day at church last week. Her mind is so full of lies and evil. She imagines things that are not true!"

Mary Warren shook her head violently. "No, it was your specter I saw that night in prison, and it matters not if you call yourself Goody Darling or Downing. It was you I saw! It was you alone who pricked me with your fingers covered in blood."

George Burroughs, Rebecca Nurse, and Elizabeth Proctor offered no words other than "not guilty" when asked for their pleas. They had been worn down by previous accusations from the afflicted girls. Within seconds, the magistrate pounded his gavel upon the table, announcing that we would all await trial in prison.

I fell to my knees, and Elizabeth Proctor helped me stand and took me by the hand. Our fates linked us through the malicious testimony of Mary Warren. I looked around the courtroom for John. My dear husband was held back as I was led away with the others. It had been one score and four years since I had seen the inside of the Ipswich Gaol. Now it would be my wretched home while storms of accusations continued to destroy all in their path.

We descended several prison steps into the dank pit, the same squalid conditions I knew in my youth. The prisoners, now more numerous, were of two kinds: those who vehemently proclaimed their innocence and those who admitted to witchcraft so their lives would be spared. A few others were deranged, and some were thought to dabble in black magic. The innocent declared they could never confess to the heinous charge of being in allegiance with Satan. Their eternal souls were more precious than life itself. They would die as martyrs because of their bravery and honesty rather than suffer the fiery and eternal rebuke from heaven.

Days turned into weeks and then months. I should have been at home teaching my children, tending to the servants' work and labor on our farm alongside my husband. John and the other families suffered along with those of us in prison. They had to pay the warden and his wife a high price for each meal and for the few privileges we were allowed—a space close to a window, fresh straw, or a visit from a servant to deliver necessary items. Even letters carried a substantial cost. I was not aware of the many kind and respectable people who helped in some way during my time in prison. Often their deeds were kept silent for fear they too might be accused.

New prisoners came in every few days, and upon learning the fates of the other inmates, had little encouragement of a quick release.

Mary Green and Phoebe Day became my closest companions. We tried to keep each other's spirits encouraged.

Rachel Clinton lay silently in the straw most of the day, with no one from the outside to care about her. She appeared to sleep while the rest of us prayed, sang, and held one another. Rachel's years of wretched treatment had taken a toll on her mind and spirit. It was difficult for me to ignore her like the others did, as I remembered how Father had taken pity on her. When I caught her eye, the slightest smile would come to her face, and she would say, "Richard Braybrooke was a good man ... a good man."

As summer ended and the cooler nights of fall arrived, the futility of our pleas and those of our loved ones at home were met with an eerie silence. Few new prisoners joined us, and our days of misery seemed never-ending as we shared this uncommon sisterhood.

Most of us were well aware that the impending winter would soon be upon us. This bone-chilling vermin pit that was our home would be our common grave if our trials delayed much longer. Our moans and coughs were a constant reminder of our plight.

One morning, I awoke to the sound of a wretched cough. Poor old Hanah Brumidge was suffering through another spasm. She had become dreadfully weakened and could not sit upright on her own. I crawled quietly over to her side;

Goodwife Vinson was already there, and we lifted her body to a more comfortable position. Before I could move away, she coughed so violently that her bloody phlegm flew onto my collar. Her coughs continued while I tried to wipe off the foul mess.

Goody Vinson put her hand on my arm and looked into my eyes. Tears stained her drawn face. "Mehitabel, if this misery continues, some evening we will all enter into our sleep, but we will not all wake up the next morning." Her words of doom sent shivers down my spine.

I signaled all the women who were nearby to come sit near Goodwife Vinson. Soon, nine of us hunched together on the straw in our corner.

"Before long, we will all suffer like Hanah if we are not released from this living tomb," I said. "We have often discussed the need to contact the authorities in Boston. The time has come for us to write a letter to the governor. Goody Greene, will you approach the guard and ask for writing paper and ink? Tell them my husband, John, will pay him on his next visit."

Goody Greene left the group to beg for the items.

"Sisters, we all have heard the governor has suspended the court proceedings, and none of us will be brought to trial until after January or February," I said. "December's hostile winds will soon be upon us."

Hanah clutched her jaw and moaned. "The throbbing of my rotting teeth brings me enough misery without the thought of the winter's icy shivers wreaking terror over my body."

Goody Greene rejoined us with the parchment and quill. "Who amongst us has the finest hand for writing?" I asked.

Before anyone had a chance to reply, a voice from close by responded, "I believe it is you, Mehitabel. Your hand is steady."

There stood Joan Penney. "I wish to add my name to your petition."

Since her arrival in September, my stepmother Joan Penney was viewed with skepticism. Well-known healers like her were now considered suspect and possible dabblers in sorcery. Joan's medicines were reported by some to produce extraordinary and violent effects. Eventually, the other prisoners had learned to calm their fears about Joan, but she had still remained reclusive.

Goodwife Vinson smiled at her now. "Joan, of course. The letter will be better received if we have more names. You are welcome to join us. Come sit next to me."

Slowly, even I was beginning to feel some compassion for Joan. Watching her sorrow these past two months brought back relentless memories of our shared suffering through the years.

I knelt on the cold ground to use the rough-hewn bench as a writing table.

"I will make my best effort to bond together our thoughts and miseries. This parchment is precious, and I must write with care."

"To the Honourable Governer and Councell and Generall Assembly now sitting at Boston: The humble petition of us whose names are subscribed, hereunto now prisoners at Ipswich, humbly sheweth that some of us have Lyen in the prison many monthes, and some of us many weekes, who are charged with witchcraft, and not being consciouse to our selves of any guilt of that nature lying upon our consciences; our earnest request is that seing the winter is soe far come on that it can not be exspected that we should be tryed during this winter season, that we may be released out of prison for the present upon Bayle to answer what we are charged with in the Spring. For we are not in this unwilling nor afrayed to abide the tryall before any Judicature apoynted in convenient season of any crime of that nature; we hope you will put on the bowells of compassion soe far as to concider of our suffering condicion in the present state we are in, being like to perish with cold in lying longer in prison in this cold season of the yeare, some of us being aged either about or nere four score, some though younger yet being with Child, and one giving suck to a child not ten weekes old yet, and all of us weake and infirme at the best, and one fettered with irons this halfe yeare and all most distroyed with soe long an Imprisonment: Thus hoping you will grant us a releas at the present that we be not left to perish in this miserable condicion we shall alwayes pray &c."

I set the quill on the ground. "Let us each sign this letter. Joan, would you begin?"

Each woman came forward to kneel and sign her name:

"Widow Penney, Widow Vincent, Widow Princ, Goodwife Greene of Havarell, the wife of Hugh Roe of Cape Anne, Mehitabel Downing, Phoebe the wife of Timothy Day, Goodwife Dicer of Piscataqua, Hanah Brumidge of Havarell, Rachel Hafield, besides thre or foure men.[1]"

So fine and sincere a plea would surely invoke the sympathy of the governor! We understood we still must stand trial but only asked that we be allowed to suffer

---

[1]	Cited from "The Petition of Ten Persons from Ipswich," Document Number 702, Library of Congress, Washington, D.C.: John Davis Batchelder Autograph Collection.

through the winter in our homes. Surely, the governor would not want to add our deaths to the scores who had suffered so unjustly.

Our letter was sent on the thirteenth of December. A reply came, not with a pardon but with blankets intended to encourage us to endure on. Our tears fell into the rough cloth, but we resolved to be strong and to help one another persevere.

# Chapter Thirty-Seven

## Winter, 1693

Darkness spread its shadowy wings over those who slumbered nearby. Weary and exhausted, I sighed and rested my head upon the wall. The soft rustle of straw near Phoebe Day let me know her night was also fitful. Discreet as the quiet river rats that frequently joined us, I moved in her direction.

"Phoebe, are you awake?" I whispered.

"Yes, come," she answered. "Rest your head against my shoulder." Few words were spoken as we slipped into a deep slumber and the heavy hours of the night crept by.

Daylight had barely entered our room the next morning when my head jerked forward. A solitary beam was shining down, illuminating the straw across from me. The first image I glimpsed was Joan. Her frail body quivered with pain, and her hollowed eyes opened. She moaned and turned to shun the light. Joan's time was near, and there was nothing I could do to hinder it.

I stretched and slowly sat upright. Phoebe's eyes were also locked in on Joan's withering form. "Phoebe, what could be the reason God chose each person here to suffer but did not choose others? I have pondered that question and can find no reason. You and I have known most of these women and men since we were wee children. I know that rain falls upon the just and the unjust, but the evil of the accusers and their lies are beyond my understanding. Why does God allow such injustice?"

Phoebe glanced at my face then lovingly took my hand and embraced it. "Mehitabel, we are like a farmer's field. God plows and tills the soil of our souls to produce a crop and to prepare us for greater fruitfulness. We must turn our eyes away from our current sorrows and fix them on God's discipline in our lives."

"Ah, Phoebe, what you speak of is too great a mystery. I ask that God hurries through this season in my life so that I won't leave this prison cell as a madwoman … or a dead one."

"Mehitabel, God's discipline, even in this prison cell, is always to prepare us for blessing, and blessing must be rightly received. Consider that food not digested is a bane, not a blessing. Disciplines not rightly received sour rather than sweeten our soul."

"So, you're saying that we must embrace God's unexplained providences with a song in these prison walls in order to please Him? Phoebe, I have tried to act kindly toward Joan since she entered prison, but I confess that my heart is still swollen with hatred toward her. I often wonder of the reason for her being here, near death. Could it be that she deserves God's punishment for her wickedness toward me?"

Phoebe continued to stroke my hand the way a mother would. "Mehitabel, that is only for God to know. We must take God's promises to heart. We all have so precious little time to make our hearts right before God ... and you with Joan. The road to mercy for you is right here before you."

The sudden stamping of feet upon the frozen ground outside roused the other prisoners. The morning twinges of pain radiated through their stiff bodies as they rose. Most prisoners desired to be among the first to taste the fresh water before it was mixed into the putrid bucket in the center of the room.

I embraced Phoebe and thanked her for such wisdom. After we drank water and ate the stale bread, some of us gathered near the window. Those of us who could read took turns reciting from God's Word, while others sat in their dark corners and listened. Mary Dicer read from Psalms and then passed the tattered Bible to me. I opened to the book of Genesis and read aloud the story of Joseph. Joseph, a son of Jacob, had been unjustly thrown into the pits of a jail. I came to these words: *But as for you, ye thought evil against me; but God meant it unto good, to bring to pass, as it is this day, to save much people alive.*

I stopped reading, not able to continue. This verse spoke the reason I was here in prison with Joan. My bitterness toward her had smoldered inside me all these years, but God brought us together in prison to heal our spiritual and emotional wounds. I pondered this insight, but I was not fully prepared to follow through on any path of mercy and forgiveness.

The winds screamed throughout the following night, but a high-pitched whistle from the crack in the wall above me lulled me to sleep. Suddenly, an eerie feeling caused me to awaken, and I heard what I thought was Joan's voice. As the fog of my sleep cleared, I knew the voice wasn't real, but I knew also that it was not the wind. It came from the end of a dream, and the events were incredibly vivid. Joan had been stroking my hair, and I was much younger. I had just given birth to Nathaniel, and Joan was tending to me in a loving, motherly way. She held my child and told him he was the most beautiful baby she had ever seen. She said, "You are the most beautiful baby, except for when your mother was a wee one."

That dream haunted me. Could God be revealing to me that Joan had been cursed far worse than I? She was not only childless but had been sinned against by my father. And because of her bitterness, the one child she had been given to raise had been driven away, and she was now alone in life. God then reminded me of His command to care for the widow—the Widow Penney.

The brutal morning chill was much the same as I felt every day. Fog poured in through every crack and chink of the prison walls. But this morning I also felt the presence of God. He wrapped His arms around me, giving warmth to my body and my soul, and I knew now that He had shown me the path to finally break my lifelong curse. I sensed the push of His hand for me to lie next to Joan and cover her with my blankets. She must have felt the stir, for she turned to me and smiled. She then covered me with the edges and pulled me next to her to share the warmth. Tears streamed gently down our cheeks.

# CHAPTER THIRTY-EIGHT

I stayed at Joan's side for hours. Our eyes met with the glow of forgiveness. How I regretted the countless years when we considered only our individual plights and not one another's. I resolved to regard Joan as a true mother as we lived out the rest of our time here on earth. If we perished today, I was confident we could stand before God and receive His greeting of pleasure.

Our reconciliation seemed to make the following days more bearable for all. God's mercy also sent a period of unusual warmth to New England. Most of us were regularly tended by our families, while others suffered through the sparse meals of bread and water from the warden's wife. These more unfortunates worried they would perish even if all were released. No one would be allowed to leave the prison until they paid the bills for their meals and even their shackles.

The claws of winter slowly released their grip upon Ipswich. Outside the barred window, a lone blackbird serenaded with a sweet and bright melody. He announced the world would soon come out of hibernation. Terror had worn out its welcome.

Joining in the blackbird's celebration one early spring morning were voices echoing from a distance. The sounds from the crowd came closer, and our hearts quickened. Many of us began to hear our names called out. Then, the voice I cherished most: "Mehitabel! You are to be released!"

I hurried to meet John but then glanced back to find Joan, who was looking down at the straw floor. Other women heard the same words from their husbands, but no one called for her. "Joan, you are to come with us if we are all pardoned. John will understand."

Joan winced in pain as she shuffled to her feet. "It will be God's gracious mercy for us all if we are released."

Just then Joan's name was called out by the warden, signaling her release. We held each other and wept tears of gladness. Joan wiped her cheeks with her gray, soiled apron. "Our fates as we come into this world and depart are quite similar, are they not? Thank you, Mehitabel, my child. I surely don't deserve your kindness."

John's eyes widened when he entered the prison and saw Joan and me standing together, with my arm around her. He didn't need to be told: our good and merciful God had lifted my curse. My family would be reunited at last.

John walked up to us, and I put my other arm around him. "Mehitabel," he said, his breath coming in short spurts. "The governor's pardon has come through at last. Finally, through so many petitions and the good work of our dear William Hubbard, the court has seen the injustice. There will not be a trial. Come, let us leave at once, and do not set your eyes to look back. You are to come home to your children."

This dark and mysterious season had come to an end. I was overjoyed by a beam of heavenly light that passed through me like a warm ocean wave. I ached to see my children and my home after these seven months in prison.

I held onto Joan's arm as I led her up the creaking stairs and spoke to my husband. "Joan is to come home with us. She needs to be with her family, so we can tend to her and restore her health. These walls have taken a severe toll on her."

John also held onto Joan. We stood at the top for a moment so our weak eyes could adjust to the late winter brightness. As we escorted her to the cart, Joan seemed to stand taller with the knowledge that her remaining years would not be uncertain and harsh as she had feared. Here, in the twilight of her life, she would be the mother and grandmother God had always planned her to be.

# CHAPTER THIRTY-NINE

The year Joan lived with us after our release from prison would be her last. Like other widows who suffered the shame and physical cruelties of prison, Joan lost her farm. Her possessions were sold off by Thomas Penney's spiteful children. Not a table, spoon, or linen remained. At age seventy-two, Joan never talked to us about her financial ruin, and John and I knew it was futile to go to the courts on her behalf.

We tried to make Joan feel like an honored grandmother in our home. Our boys would carry her to the chair near the fireplace, and she would stroke their hair and cheeks in gratitude.

Life in Ipswich was forever changed, and so many lives and estates lay in ruin. Ipswich's righteous and honorable people aligned themselves with those who were poorly treated. The unjust imprisonment of hundreds and the deaths of the twenty accused continued to divide the town.

A special bond grew between those of us who had suffered. We had been posted as criminals, taunted with aspersion, and forbidden the counsel of law. Our words of defense had been twisted into a semblance of condemnation, but we were able to show genuine nobility. We counted our lives not dear to us but instead considered only the opinion of our Savior as most precious. Our only hope for eternal salvation was to stand as innocent in the eyes of God. To admit to the heinous sin of aligning with the Devil would have separated us for eternity from our Creator.

Those who had falsely accused their neighbors or remained silent were overwhelmed by shame that hung like a grindstone on their countenance. So much could have been done to stop the hysteria, but everyone seemed to walk in a thick cloud of delusion and fear. I bore my own shame for my hesitancy to aid those like the Proctors, who had been falsely accused. John Proctor was hanged, but Elizabeth was spared because she was with child. There was little consolation in the memory of my clumsy attempt to bring Mary Warren into accountability.

In the months that followed the trials, some townsfolk lied when asked about their false accusations. Others feigned ignorance and pretended to recall nothing of their testimony. How we all wished to put this nightmare behind us and move on, but the damage and suffering were too deep.

Mary Warren left the area, as no one would welcome her as a servant in their home. Mr. Parris and his family soon left Salem Village, and he never pastored again. Our pastor, Reverend Hubbard, chose an unfortunate second wife after the death of Mistress Hubbard. His new wife was considered coarse and far below his station in life. No one approved of her, although most tried to be kind in gratitude for all Reverend Hubbard had done for the accused.

One midsummer day, I peeked out the door to observe if the steady rains had ceased. I noted a momentary hint of blue in the sky and looked back at Joan sitting in her chair. "Joan, would you like to sit outside and enjoy the cooler air?"

"No, Mehitabel, but come sit next to me." Joan pointed to the bench close to her and began to study me intently. "Mehitabel, tell me. Do you have any memories of when you were a young girl? Tell me about our pleasant times together. My mind has grown so forgetful."

In earlier years, my only response would have been, "There were none! When I was a child, you hated me!"

Instead, I answered with the one pleasant memory I treasured. "Mother, I remember how you would teach me about plants and barks on trips to the forest. You were considered to be the best healer in Ipswich. You knew so many remedies, and the townspeople would seek you out for advice. I also recall the herbs and spices like sage, parsley, and rosemary that you would grow in your lovely garden. Our food always had an appealing aroma and taste."

Joan smiled and quickly added, "Oh, I remember how Richard loved the smell of food when he entered the house, how the first thing he would say was, 'Mother has been tending to my dinner in her special way. What is your secret today, my dear?' You and I would laugh and tell him the special spice was our love."

At that moment, I realized Joan no longer remembered herself as a bitter and unkind wife or mother. Her mind had given her the gift to forget the hurts of the past. She recalled her life the way she wished it had been. An old mind grown feeble and worn can at times be a blessing for all.

It was in this manner we spent the rest of Joan's months. I learned to embellish the few memories that were sweet-natured and retell them again and again. She would smile and recite from Second Corinthians 13:11, the only passage of Scripture she could recall: *Be perfect, be of good comfort, be of one mind, live in peace; and the God of love and peace shall be with you.*

*I now bid farewell to you, Joan, as you enter God's eternal Kingdom.* How much sweeter and at peace our lives could have been! If only we had resolved long ago to smother the curse that burdened our family all those years. I praised God that He gave me grace and mercy to seal the curse and be redeemed. No longer would I live in lamentable regret and with the shame of my past. Like the great patriarch Joseph, my time in prison was used for good. *I now make a holy vow to embrace these words as I live the rest of my years. Rest in peace, Joan ... my mother.*

# CHAPTER FORTY

# JUNE 1714

It is always a melancholy time when a child leaves home. Nathaniel, our second youngest son, his wife Margaret, and our new grandchild would soon leave for a new territory near Springfield in the Massachusetts Colony where the land was said to be more suitable for farming. He had been offered a teaching opportunity in addition to fifty acres of land.

Nathaniel had always been different, with books and intellectual pursuits his greatest desire. He and Margaret had grown weary of the dark, heavy spirit that continued to plague our towns from the days of accusations. We shared their weariness and rejoiced in the promise of their new adventure.

Nathaniel was named after Mistress Hubbard's learned and esteemed father, Nathaniel Rogers. My dear husband, John, had been cared for by the Reverend Rogers when his parents returned to England. It was, thus, appropriate that my Nathaniel possessed an adventurous spirit like John's father, Emanuel.

The esteemed Hubbard, Pynchon, and Rogers families were woven together with ours by the marriage of our son Nathaniel Downing and Margaret Hubbard. Such an honor could not have brought more happiness. Reverend and Mistress Hubbard had departed this earth, but surely they smiled down from the heavens to see their granddaughter married to our son.

It gave John and me great comfort that our other three children chose to stay near. Our dear sons John and David were given much of the old Braybrooke farm, in hopes the land might knit their families to Ipswich and Gloucester. Our son Charles died of a high fever ten years ago.

Sarah married Thomas Lufkin, who was like another son to John and me. I recalled our worries when the Lufkins proposed that Thomas break his promise of marriage to Sarah after I was accused of witchcraft. The good Reverend William Hubbard intervened, and the marriage took place while I was still in prison. What could have been used to cause bitterness in our families instead bound us closer. Thomas referred to us as his "revered Father and Mother." Such an honorable tribute they had given us in our old age!

The distressing cries of my grandchild announced Nathaniel and his family's arrival to our home and that his departure day had finally come. Our other children and their families had already arrived to say their goodbyes.

"Do you hear how baby Margaret does not want to leave her grandmother? I believe the babe is saying that her parents may leave, but she will stay with Grandmother Hetty in Ipswich." I smiled as I made jest but knew if she could speak, that surely was what she would say.

Our beloved grandchild was also named for Mistress Margaret Hubbard. Each time I gazed upon baby Margaret, the memory of Mistress Margaret Hubbard came to mind and blessed me. John and I were getting up in age. This could be my last time ever again to hold this precious child.

Nathaniel knelt in front of my chair for his final goodbyes. "Mother, we shall leave in a few moments to join our fellow travelers, but Margaret and I have something to present to you, which will require forgiveness."

I was puzzled because I could recall no offense.

Nathaniel continued, "About a month ago, I resolved to find my way into the town books, and I made the decision to remove these."

Nathaniel handed me a carefully wrapped set of papers with frayed edges. As I loosened the ribbon, it became evident the papers were ones I had never actually seen, yet each word had been etched on my soul. Nathaniel looked at his brothers and sister with confidence, and by their reactions, I knew all had been complicit.

"Mother, we all know about the terrible times so many endured. The lies and atrocities brought great shame to all in New England. So many innocents walked about as if in a dark cloud of despair, not knowing what to do. You, dear Mother, should not have to bear the disgrace of the false accusations made against you so long ago."

I opened the scrolls to read the documents:

The first accusation by my accuser …

The warrant for my arrest …

The listing of my prison costs …

All there.

"We have all made a pledge that the name of Mehitabel Downing shall be honored in Ipswich. You and your descendants can live and die proudly without the contamination of others' sins against you. Soon, no one will remember the witchcraft hysteria, and this will all be forgotten. And so it ends here for our family."

Tears welled up in my eyes, and my hands became weak and trembled as I held these papers torn from the record books. "Children, I think often of those turbulent times where all who lived in Essex County were not safe from the

Devil's seeds of hysteria. Houses of people filled with the doleful shrieks of their children and servants tormented by some invisible hand. Yet, while I was but one of the hundreds accused, I knew of God's unconditional love for me. I knew you, my precious ones, suffered with me. You knew the truth of my innocence and the great injustice done to so many."

I put my arm through John's and gazed at my dear husband's face before looking back at my offspring. "In my life, through all the storms and curses that pierced my heart, there was always at least one person who loved me with an intensity that only God can bestow. My father; Reverend and Mistress Hubbard; my husband, John, and now you my children, and your spouses. All of you have been that God-given person to me."

I rolled up the papers and pressed them into Nathaniel's hands. "I look at baby Margaret and think of the legacy left to her as I read these papers. Her grandfather, Reverend Hubbard, saved many a person here in Ipswich because of his wisdom and courage. I would not want my children and the Hubbards' grandchildren to have this legacy passed down to them."

Nathaniel understood that I agreed with his decision. The Downings' secret would be carried to our graves. The reign of Satan and his curse upon our generations had now ceased.

Margaret and Nathaniel said their farewells to all, amid the tears and well-wishes. My son came to me for our final embrace. When I had the strength to release him, he turned and walked to the fireplace and rested the scrolls upon the gently flickering flames.

John and I sat while the others stood silently and looked on as the flames devoured the papers. While the final ashes smoldered, I pondered why so many chose to believe Satan's lies. It suited them to do so because their own families were consumed with hate and greed. Our town had almost been entirely consumed by the Great Deceiver.

The scrolls were but ash when my son departed with his two dear Margarets. The roots of my curse were consumed by the flames, and my vindication in both the eyes of men and God was complete. My adversary the Devil walked about like a roaring lion, seeking me to devour, but God protected me with His mercy and allowed me to fight back.

I was forgiven. I had finally been redeemed.

# AUTHOR'S NOTE

The story of Mehitabel Braybrooke Downing emerged from the earliest village and court records of Ipswich, Massachusetts. Mehitabel's life began in 1652 as the illegitimate child born from her father's affair with his indentured servant. After being whipped for fornication, Richard Braybrooke brought the child home and raised her in his household. His wife, Joan, who could not have children of her own, had a contemptuous relationship with her stepdaughter. Life in the Braybrooke household could not have been easy for Mehitabel.

Mehitabel's story is remarkable as her foibles and crimes produced numerous records from the time of her birth to the early 1700s. Unlike the aristocracy and more prominent Puritans, people like Mehitabel typically left few journals or diaries, although she is one of the signers of the "Ten Persons of Ipswich Letter" from the Salem Witchcraft period. A Puritan woman of her status might have left only a birth, marriage, or a death record.

The parents of John Downing, Mehitabel's husband, were of the gentry class and well educated. Emanuel and Lucy Downing left many letters giving researchers insightful historical background about Ipswich's earliest years. Lucy Downing was the sister of John Winthrop, governor of the Massachusetts Bay Colony. Lucy's letters show her desire to promote the interest of her eldest son, George, above all of her other children. The only reference to John Downing in her letters was when she sent her regards to "little Jack." We can only hope she was referring to her young son, John, who was left behind in the colonies when Lucy and Emanuel returned to England to follow George, her esteemed and politically connected son.

Cold hard facts don't make an interesting story on their own. If I had based this story only on the surviving records, Mehitabel's character would reflect the descriptors from her court records: "bastard child, arsonist, drunk, accused witch." She would likely be considered the original "Puritan bad girl," but this would reveal a lack of understanding of the Puritan culture and dismissal of the complexities of human nature. A more emotionally intriguing portrayal was in order.

This novel doesn't cater to modern sensibilities and beliefs but instead attempts to accurately explain the thinking and customs of a struggling group of

Puritans. For example, I could have woven in a friendly Native American friend for Mehitabel to promote today's multiculturalism, but that would not have been true to the historical period. The Puritans, with good reason, were fearful of the Indians and would have never considered issues such as Native Americans' land ownership. They were Puritans and thought it was God's providence that brought them to New England.

This book does not overemphasize the Salem Witchcraft Trials and the topic of witchcraft in general. There are many books on Salem's witchcraft history and well-written historical novels that cover the year of 1692. While Mehitabel was accused of witchcraft in June of 1692, she did not live in Salem Village, the epicenter of the hysteria. Ipswich bordered Salem Village, which was renamed Danvers a few years after the trials. Historians agree that none of the twenty men and women executed for the practice of witchcraft were guilty of that crime. I included no gratuitous casting of spells or witchery out of respect for the two hundred innocent people accused during the Salem Witchcraft Trials.

# Historical Characters

**Mr. John Appleton** served for many years as Deputy to the General Court, Treasurer of Essex County, and as one of the Justices of the Inferior Court of Pleas. He was awarded the rank of Captain in the military. (1622-Nov. 4, 1699)

**Mr. Samuel Appleton,** the brother of John Appleton, was a military and government leader in the Massachusetts Bay Colony. He was a commander of the Massachusetts militia during King Phillip's War and led troops during the attack on Hatfield, Massachusetts, and the Great Swamp Fight. He also held numerous positions in government and was an opponent of Governor Sir Edmund Andros. (1625-May 15, 1696)

**John Beare** was the nephew of Richard Braybrooke. He lived with the Braybrooke family, and Richard willed him land in Denham. (1648-1722)

**Timothy, Edward, and Goody Bragg** were Ipswich residents who testified against Mehitabel in her arson case of 1668.

**Mehitabel Downing Braybrooke** was born in 1652 in Ipswich, Massachusetts. While there is no birth record for Mehitabel, the Essex Court Records note that Richard Braybrooke was guilty of fornication with his servant. His sentence was to receive a whipping, but his servant's punishment was delayed until "after her travail." The judgment also mentioned that Richard was to raise the child as his own. Richard was married to Joan Edyss at the time of Mehitabel's birth.

Mehitabel was sent off as a servant in the home of Jacob Perkins. "Sending off" was used by Puritans not only as a form of discipline but as a sort of apprenticeship to learn adult work skills and manners.

Mehitabel shows up in the Essex Court Records in August 1668 on the charge of arson. A great deal of testimony on this case has survived and shows Mehitabel to be a young lady who lacks common sense. Some of the court testimony reveals that Joan described Mehitabel to neighbors as "a liar, a thief, and an unchaste creature." It is evident that Joan held Mehitabel in contempt.

At that time in the colonies, a conviction of arson was a capital murder offense. The magistrate declared Mehitabel guilty of "extreme carelessness, if not willfully burning the house." She was whipped and had to pay a fine of £40.

Mehitabel Downing was one of almost two hundred people accused of witchcraft during the Salem Hysteria in 1692. No grave or record of her death has been located, but unsourced histories indicate she died in 1723.

**Richard Braybrooke** was Mehitabel's father. Essex Court records indicate he was found guilty of "fornication" with his indentured servant and was severely whipped. The courts required Richard to raise Mehitabel.

Richard was born in England and came to Ipswich sometime in the 1630s. He was a prosperous landowner and freeman in Ipswich. (1613-November 1681)

**Hanah Brumidge** and **Phoebe Day** were two of Mehitabel's fellow prisoners in the Ipswich jail in 1692, and they also signed "The Ten Prisoners of Ipswich" letter.

**Major Daniel Dennison** held a number of important positions in the early years of the colony. He was a military leader, Speaker of the House, Secretary of the Massachusetts Colony, and the justice of the quarterly and general courts in Essex County. (1612-1583)

**Emanuel Downing,** John Downing's father, was born August 12, 1585, in Ipswich, England. He was a barrister of the Inner Temple and represented the Massachusetts Bay Colony before the Privy Council in London. Emanuel's first wife, Anne Ware, the mother of his first three children, died in 1621. His second wife was Lucy Winthrop.

Emanuel and Lucy settled in Salem and purchased three hundred acres of land in Peabody at Proctor's Crossing. The Downings built a house and named it Groton after Lucy's childhood home in England.

Emanuel made nine trips back to England to represent the interests of the colonies. In 1645, while he was in England, the chimney of their house caught fire, and the entire house was consumed. Upon his return, Emanuel purchased a house on Essex Street and lived there until he and Lucy returned to England in 1656.

Emanuel practiced law in Scotland until his death in 1660. He is buried in Westminster in London near Trafalgar Square at St. Martin-in-the-Fields Churchyard. (1585-1660)

### Children of John and Mehitabel Downing:

Charles 1670-1690

Sarah 1673-1724

John Jr. 1674-1747

David 1678-1723

Nathaniel 1679-1740

Richard 1683-1702

**Sir George Downing** was a brother of John Downing and an Anglo-Irish preacher, soldier, statesman, diplomat, turncoat, and spy, after whom Downing Street in London is named. As Treasury Secretary, he is credited with instituting major reforms in public finance. His influence on the passage and substance of the mercantilist Navigation Acts was substantial. The Acts strengthened English commercial and naval power, contributing to the security of the English state and its ability to project its power abroad. More than any other man, George Downing was responsible for arranging the acquisition of New York from the Dutch and is remembered there in the name of Downing Street in Manhattan and Downing Street in Brooklyn.

The Puritans in the American colony considered George Downing a scoundrel. He quickly switched his alliances back to the King when Cromwell fell from power, and he blamed the "principles sucked in" during his time in the American colonies and now "saw the error." He handed over some secret documents to the king as proof of his good intentions. The author published an article about him for the New England Historical Society: http://www.newenglandhistoricalsociety. com/massachusetts-scoundrel-downing-street-named/ (1623-22 July 1684)

**James Downing** was John Downing's half-brother from Emanuel's first marriage in England to Anne Ware. Emanuel appeared to be somewhat disappointed with James and referred to his writing as "scribbling nonsense." (1616-?)

**John Downing** was born to Emanuel and Lucy Winthrop Downing in 1640 in Ipswich, Massachusetts. He was one of their youngest children and remained in the colonies with most of his siblings when his parents returned to England.

John was given the title of "planter" in the town records, which indicates he owned over three hundred acres of land. Some genealogists confuse him with a few other men named John Downing written about in Massachusetts history. Most of the historical evidence and traditional genealogies indicate that John Downing, son of Emanuel, was indeed the man who married Mehitabel Braybrooke.

The year of John's death is not certain but is estimated to be 1714.

**Alice Ellys** was the indentured servant of Richard Braybrooke and was his partner in fornication. She was to be whipped "after her travail" and disappears from history after that event.

**Mr. John Endicott** was one of the founders of the Massachusetts Bay Colony. He was vehemently opposed to the Quakers and was passionate about the need to convert the Native American populations to Christianity. (1600-1665)

**Samuel Giddings** was a resident of Ipswich, one of the men who testified that he saw Mehitabel Downing lying drunk with the swine. (1645-1692)

**Rachel Clinton Haffield** lived a rather tragic life. She married Lawrence Clinton, a deceitful younger man who swindled her out of her inheritance. He had several children with another woman, but the courts would not grant Rachel a divorce. Destitute, Rachel was forced to beg in Ipswich and was an easy target when the witchcraft accusations began. She was one of the "ten persons of Ipswich." (1629-1694/95)

**Margaret Downing Pynchon** was the granddaughter of Reverend William and Margaret (Mary) Hubbard and wife of Nathaniel Downing, John and Mehitabel's son. (1680-1740)

**Reverend William Hubbard** was a clergyman and historian in Ipswich, Massachusetts, after he graduated from Harvard College in 1642. He was the pastor of the Puritan/Congregational church in Ipswich until the year before his death. Hubbard wrote *A History of New England* and *A Narrative of Trouble with the Indians*, two of the first histories of early America. (1621-1704)

**Thomas Lufkin** was the husband of Sarah Downing, whom he married in December 1692. He was a member of one of the founding families of Ipswich. (1668-1747)

**Rebecca Nurse, George Burroughs, Elizabeth Proctor** were accused by Mary Warren of witchcraft along with Mehitabel Downing on June 1, 1692. *Abigail Hobbs and Mary Warren vs. George Burroughs et al.*

**Joan Braybrooke Penney** was the wife of Richard Braybrooke. She was childless, a great shame for most women throughout history. Court records reveal that Joan held Mehitabel in disdain and talked about her in a most unflattering way to the village women.

After the death of Thomas Penney, her second husband, Joan was accused of witchcraft by Zebulon Hill. Her court records still exist, including a newly discovered one that reveals her as the woman who recited the Lord's Prayer without error. Although this feat was said to be impossible for a real witch, it made no difference to the magistrates who allowed her to languish in prison for months. (1615-1693)

**Thomas Penney** was the second husband of Joan Braybrooke. He died in early 1692, and his death left Joan vulnerable to witchcraft accusations. (1600-1692)

**Abraham and Hannah Perkins** were residents of Ipswich, and Abraham was the brother of Jacob Perkins.

**Jacob and Sarah Perkins** were the owners of the home in Ipswich that Mehitabel set on fire in 1668.

**King Phillip** was the main leader of the armed conflict between Native American inhabitants of present-day New England and English colonists and their Native American allies in 1675–78. **Metacomet** adopted the English name "King Phillip" in honor of the previously friendly relations between his father and the original Mayflower Pilgrims.

**Elizabeth Proctor** was the wife of John Proctor and was accused and convicted of witchcraft. Her sentence was delayed because of her pregnancy, and she escaped hanging when the witchcraft hysteria ended. (1650-after 1710)

**John Proctor** was accused by Mary Warren and hanged for witchcraft in 1692. The Proctors rented the tavern built by Emanuel Downing. John was inaccurately portrayed in Arthur Miller's "The Crucible" as the former lover of Abigail, the niece of Reverend Parris. John Proctor was in his sixties, and Abigail was just eleven, making a romantic relationship unlikely. (1631-1692)

**Margaret Rogers Hubbard**, the daughter of Reverend Nathaniel Rogers, was born in Ipswich and was the wife of William Hubbard. Margaret was held in high esteem especially in contrast to William's second wife, who was deemed unworthy due to her low status in Ipswich. (1628-1690)

**Nathaniel Rogers** was an early minister in Ipswich and father of Margaret Hubbard, wife of William Hubbard. (1598-1655)

**Job Smith** was a resident of Ipswich and one of the men who testified that he saw Mehitabel Downing lying drunk with the swine. 1663-?

**Samuel Stone** was a deacon and selectman in Essex County. (1636-1693)

**Goodwife Rachel Vinson** was one of Mehitabel's fellow prisoners in the Ipswich jail in 1692 and also signed "The Ten Prisoners of Ipswich" letter.

**Mary Warren** was twenty years old when she became one of the most rigorous accusers—and also a defender and confessor, a unique role among the accusing girls of Salem Village. She was the servant of John and Elizabeth Proctor and encountered much resistance from the two regarding her participation in the trials. Most significant, Mary introduced the possibility of fraud on the part of the accusing girls when she stated that they "did but dissemble." Mary accused Goody (Mehitabel) Downing, John Proctor, George Burroughs and Rebecca Nurse of witchcraft on June 1, 1692. After her own confession, Mary more actively participated in the accusations, including those against the Proctors. She was released from jail in June 1692. (1673-1697 or 1709)

**Thomas Wells** was a freeman and yeoman in Ipswich who came from England in 1635. (1605-1666)

**Governor John Winthrop** was the Governor of the Massachusetts colony and brother of Lucy Downing. He brought the first group of Puritans to the Massachusetts Bay Colony on "the Winthrop fleet." (1587-1649)

**Obadiah Woods** was the husband of Hazelelponah and an owner of a tavern or "ordinary" in Ipswich. (?-1712)

**Hazelelponah Woods** was the oldest daughter of Balthazar and Hannah Willix. In 1648, her mother was attacked on the road leading from Dover to Exeter and was robbed and murdered. Her body was thrown into the river. Balthazar became despondent and moved the family to Salisbury. Hazelelponah was sent into service, as was typical for many young women of that time. She met and married John Gee.

John Gee was a fisherman but was lost at sea on Dec. 27, 1669. Hazelelponah and their five children moved to Boston where she met Obadiah Wood, a widower with ten children.

Obadiah and Hazelelponah married and were proprietors of an ordinary (tavern) in Ipswich. They added another ten children during their years of marriage. This remarkable woman survived her second husband and died in Ipswich in 1714 at the age of 79. Her grave is located in the Old North Burying Ground in Ipswich, Massachusetts. (1636-1714)

Made in the USA
Columbia, SC
25 April 2020